I0533673

DEATH IMITATING *ART*

a novel by

RICH J. STONE

glarm
ink
New York, New York

Copyright © 2008 Rich J. Stone

All rights reserved. No part of this publication may be reproduced, stored in a retrieval system or transmitted in any form or by any means, electronic, mechanical, photocopying, recording or otherwise, without the prior written permission of the publisher.

ISBN: 0981560903

EAN-13: 9780981560908

Published by Glarm Ink

Printed in the United States of America

For Quiche and Thomas

ACKNOWLEDGMENTS

The author wishes to thank the following: Nahvae Frost, Quiche Stone, Greg Sanders, Larry Trivieri, Joan Black, Ann Kruse, Patricia Foulke, Jeanette Ryan, Paul Milberg, Steven Solomon, and Mom & Dad.

DEATH IMITATING *ART*

CHAPTER ONE

THERE WAS A SPLATTER on West Broadway. Almost looked like Spin Art. Except the medium wasn't paint and paper—it was entrails and asphalt.

The ambulance had already come and gone. A uniformed NYPD cop was collecting statements. A striking brunette was being interviewed. She carried herself well despite the fact that a couple of artsy, ultra-trendy SoHo gallery types were wildly gesticulating and pointing fingers at her the whole time. I was tempted to move in to get a closer look, and see if I could catch some of the conversation; but there was just one thing preventing me: I really didn't give a shit. It was cutting into valuable drinking time. I kept right on walking, hung a left on Spring Street and made it to The Last Stand in record time.

I popped into my dank little dive of a bar, my weekday home from three in the afternoon until drunkenness prevailed. It was located in that no man's land between SoHo and Little Italy; an area that some people called "NoLita" (North of Little Italy) in a vain attempt to make it sound trendy. Vincent was behind the old wooden bar carving up limes as if they were mafia stool pigeons. Each slice of the knife drove a new gash into the bar, which fit in well with the décor. The television hanging above the bar played old sitcoms round the clock, and I could hear a faint laugh track in the background. It highlighted each of Vincent's slices, as if commenting on how pathetic it all seemed.

The only customer aside from me was a gray-bearded toothless drunk at the near end of the bar with a shot of rum in front of him. I made a quick assessment: Nasty Drunk. His red and brown slits-for-eyes followed me as I made my way to the far end of the bar and sat down on my stool. The drunk started in on me almost immediately.

"Pete used to give me a buy-back every third round. Don't expect no buy-back." His voice was hoarse, as if he'd been repeating this until he found someone who'd listen to him. I quickly re-classified him as a Ranting Drunk, although he seemed to have the range and the ability to cross over into other drunkard categories. I avoided making eye contact and pretended that I was preoccupied with the weight of the world. Not getting any action from me, he turned his fury on Vincent.

"Why ain't this Pete's shift no more?" He nearly fell off his stool and flapped his bony arms about trying to regain his balance. One of his flailing wings knocked over his shot glass. Sloppy Drunk.

"I'm sorry. I didn't mean to do that. I'm sorry, Pete. Please tell Pete I'm sorry."

Vincent uprighted the glass, wiped up the spill and poured a fresh shot of rum.

"S'okay," Vincent said, "this one's on Pete."

"Pete's a rat bastard," the old drunk said under his breath, then gulped down the shot. I was right the first time. Nasty Drunk. I made a mental note to trust my first impressions.

"How was school today, Harry?" Vincent greeted me with a tepid beer in one hand and a shot of bourbon in the other.

"Same as usual," I replied. "Erasers whizzing by my head every few seconds. Total anarchy in the classroom. But no felonies committed, so I guess I did my job."

"I ever tell you how we used to torture our substitutes?"

"Every day, Vincent. Every day."

The Nasty Drunk dozed off.

"So, who the hell is Pete?"

"Fuck should I know?" Vincent said. "Let's see how much money he's got."

"Best to let sleeping drunks lie, Vincent."

Vincent ignored my advice and started patting down the Sleepy Nasty Drunk. I quickly downed my bourbon. I can't say I approved of what Vincent was doing, but I didn't care enough to disapprove either. Vincent was a mafia wannabe. He had planned to join up with his uncles working the South Street Seaport rackets, but the Giuliani administration closed them down before Vincent got the chance. His uncles ended up in jail, or being relegated to petty theft, mostly in Queens and Jersey. Vincent's father never went the mob route. He was an accountant and Vincent hated him for it. Vincent bought The Last Stand with his legally obtained inheritance money—practically tax-free due to his father's accounting wizardry. He had a dream to use the bar as a cover for illegal activity, but the most he'd been able to muster was selling marijuana to the local artists. Big-time operator that Vincent. Big-time dreamer. So, if he wanted to roll the drunk, who was I to stop him?

Instead, I sipped my warm beer and ate some stale peanuts as my thoughts returned to West Broadway and the brunette. I only caught a glimpse of her but I remembered every detail, due in part to my photographic memory. I am probably the stupidest man in the world with an I.Q. over 170—an overrated test if there ever was one. Ever since that damn number was branded on me, I've never been able to escape it. "A 175 I.Q.? You're destined for greatness, young man. You will be another Einstein." Rather high expectations for an eight-year-old to live up to, don't you think? Now thirty years later I hear: "A substitute teacher? Why aren't you doing better things with your life?" It's a question I've heard countless times. It's a question to which I've given countless smart-ass responses. When I was fifteen, my school guidance counselor told me that with my intellectual gifts I could do anything my heart desired. At this moment in time, it desired to sit in a bar, get drunk and slowly kill off my remaining gray matter. You don't need to be Einstein to do that.

The shot glass flew off the bar and smashed against the wall, leaving a rum-stained blotch. The Drunk had awakened. Vincent grabbed him in a headlock and yanked the old boozer off his stool and out the door in one fluid motion. If Drunk Tossing were an Olympic sport, Vincent would be a gold medallist.

"How much money did he have?" I asked.

"Nothing. That's why I tossed him."

I thought about the brunette again. What was it about her? Had we met somewhere before? Probably not. Did she remind me of someone? The clouds parted. She reminded me of Julia.

I threw down my shot of bourbon, chugged the remainder of my beer and tossed some money down on the bar.

"Gonna get some pizza. You want any?"

"Going to Lombardi's?"

"No. Going west."

"Okay, get me a couple slices. So long as it's not that gourmet shit."

I hustled to the door and nearly smashed into Zane, who was on his way in carrying a still-wet canvas. No doubt, he would try to sell it to Vincent for some weed.

"Where you going, Harry?"

"Pizza. Be back soon."

I got outside and started sprinting back to West Broadway. As I ran, I heard Zane calling after me: "Get me four slices." Obviously, Zane had a cannabis-induced case of the munchies.

I ran across Lafayette Street, dodging a taxi that didn't seem to care much for pedestrians. Spring Street became trendier as I ran west, especially once I crossed Broadway. There was no longer any room on the sidewalk, so I ran in the street. Folding tables filled the sidewalks as vendors tried to sell their wares; everything artistically imaginable, from handmade jewelry to sculptures to paintings. Each of the artisans looking to make a buck, or maybe be discovered by one of the many galleries in the neighborhood. I began panting hard between Mercer and Greene Streets, and thought my heart would explode by the time I crossed Wooster. But I had only one more block to go and I continued to sprint. As I approached West Broadway, I felt my stomach clench. The bourbon was returning from whence it came and taking the beer and half-digested peanuts with it. I collapsed to my knees and started puking at the curb. My body violently gyrated as vomit spewed forth from my mouth and nose and formed a puddle on the corner of Spring and West Broadway. I considered trying to drown myself in it; but the dying-in-your-own-vomit routine hadn't been in vogue since the '70s and, therefore, wouldn't be very trendy.

My head finally ascended from the gutter. No one checked to see if I was okay. This was SoHo after all. For all anyone knew, I could have been in the midst of creating conceptual art: *Inner Rage, a color study in shades of bile*. I pushed myself up and took a less frantic pace to the splatter scene.

Everyone was gone. Not even the splatter remained. I looked around for some signs of recognition, and quickly spotted one of the ultra-trendies posing in front of the ultra-chic Reinhardt Galleries, while sucking on an ultra-carcinogenic cigarette. I scampered across the street toward her, dodging traffic.

"Excuse me," I said, still gasping for breath. "Did you see the accident?"

"Accident?" she scoffed and blew smoke in my face.

Before I could finish coughing, she took another drag

on her cigarette, let it drop to the pavement, spun herself around and entered the Galleries. I stomped out the smoldering cancer stick, and decided to follow her. The other jaded hipster greeted me as soon as I attempted to set foot inside.

"Do you have an appointment?" he asked, dripping with condescension. His nose was slightly wrinkled as if there were a bad smell. I wasn't sure if it was my puke-tinged breath, or if this was his perennial expression.

"I'm looking for the woman that the police were interviewing a little while ago. You know, out in the street?"

"I'm afraid I wasn't paying attention. And that isn't really much of a description. Good day." He tried to shut the door in my face, but my foot had already taken root in the threshold. He had insulted my powers of observation. Me and my photographic memory didn't take kindly to that.

"Perhaps a better description of her would be," I began, "a brunette woman wearing a black and gray suit, with a skirt line just above the knee. Around her neck was a multi-colored scarf, with a pewter clasp that hung slightly left of center. I believe it may have been pinned there."

The ultra-trendy interrupted me when I began describing the shadow that was cast by the heels on her shoes.

"Yes, yes. I know who you mean," he said dismissively. "Ms. Traut no longer works here."

"Do you know where I can reach her?" I asked. He said nothing, just looked down and waited for me to remove my foot.

"How does one go about getting an appointment?" I asked.

"One doesn't," he said. "One must be invited." It's hip to be rude. I pulled my foot back and the door to the ultra-full-of-itself Reinhardt Galleries closed.

Ms. Traut. Didn't ring a bell. It was a long shot anyway. I couldn't believe I actually undertook the wild goose chase to begin with. I could hear Julia's disapproving voice in my head: "Up to your old tricks again, Harrison?"

I headed back to The Last Stand, keeping careful not to step in any "puddles of art" along the way. I stopped into a non-gourmet pizza place and picked up a large pie. When I entered the bar, "Leave It to Beaver" was on the television and Zane giggled incessantly every time Eddie Haskell appeared. As we ate the pizza, I noticed Zane's painting hanging on the wall, strategically covering the rum blotch. Vincent was no art lover, but he was practical. Zane's art work was often the cheapest and most efficient solution to his bar woes. He already had one painting covering up a water stain from where a pipe had burst, and another covering up a head-sized hole in the wall where he had "broken up" a bar fight last month. When his first painting was hung, Zane was so excited he invited everyone he knew to come to a special showing at the lounge/gallery that was displaying his work. Vincent charged a five-dollar cover at the door, imposed a two-drink minimum, and took in a tidy profit at Zane's friends' expense. I took care not to let my pizza drip, lest another of Zane's paintings would be called into service.

"You know, now that I have three pieces in here, maybe I should invite some industry people," Zane thought out loud. Zane did everything out loud. There wasn't a subtle bone in his body. I could tell he was really deep in thought by the way his tongue involuntarily hung out of his mouth.

"Sounds like a good idea," I said. "Why don't you invite that Traut woman from the Reinhardt Galleries?"

Zane turned away from the television. His stoned-out expression turned solemn and he looked at me with an awe-filled bewilderment.

"You know Teresa Traut?"

I HAD A LONG CONVERSATION with Julia when I returned home that night. I told her everything that happened. I told her about the mysterious Teresa Traut and how she reminded me of her. I told her what Zane had said about her: that she was an uncompromising art appraiser who could make or break an artist. I told her about the ultra-trendies and the short conversation I had with them. I even told her about Zane's new painting. I told her all this, and she said nothing in return. I pulled Julia close to me and told her "thanks for listening."

Then I placed her urn back on the bookshelf.

CHAPTER TWO

I COULDN'T SLEEP that night. All I could think about was Teresa Traut. Images of her face kept forming in my mind and the more closely I looked, the more stunning the resemblance to Julia. Morning came all too quickly and when the phone rang at six a.m., I told the Board of Ed. registry person that I wasn't available for substitute teaching for the rest of the week.

I had a breakfast beer, got dressed and made my best attempts at shaving. I stared at myself in the bathroom mirror. A haggard, hungover has-been stared back at me. What the hell was I doing? Chasing after some ghost? And what was I planning on accomplishing anyway? Surely, Julia didn't care one way or another.

Julia is . . . was, rather, my soul mate. We'd met in one of those special classes where they separated out the high I.Q. children from the rest of the school; as if we had some sort of transmittable geek disease. We helped each other through our years of quarantine from society, both inside and outside the classroom. Julia was a 168. For some reason, our seven-point difference meant a lot; the 170 plateau was a dividing line and, as a result, far less was expected of Julia than of me. But as far as I was concerned, she was much smarter than I ever was, or ever could be. But for all Julia's smarts, she still smoked two packs of cigarettes a day. Of course, I wasn't one to condemn her. At least her cigarettes never clouded her judgment, or provided her with the need to openly retch on the sidewalk or to urinate in public. Smoking was her way of fitting in; the gateway to the "under-150s" as she would facetiously call them. I suppose that may be a reason for my drinking and bar-dwelling, but I'll save the self-psychoanalysis for another time.

There were only two listings under "Traut" in the Manhattan phone book. One Ronald Traut, and one T Traut. There was no address for T Traut, but the phone number stared me right in the face. The first three numbers were 628, an Upper East Side exchange. I quickly memorized it. Of course, there was no guarantee that this was her. She may not even live in Manhattan. She looked like an Upper East Side type, though. From the little information I had gotten about her from Zane, I surmised that she would be living in one of the following neighborhoods: the Upper East Side, Upper West Side, SoHo, TriBeCa, the West Village, or Chelsea. I was leaning toward the Upper East Side for one simple reason: artists didn't hang out there, and she seemed like the sort of person who loved art but hated artists. The Upper East Side had museums that displayed art masterpieces whose creators were long dead. Of course she lived on the Upper East Side. There was no doubt in my mind.

I gave myself a tour of SoHo that morning. I wanted to become acquainted with all of the galleries, or at least as many as I could. Silly as it seemed, I was hoping to bump into Teresa Traut by chance, and if she was out of a job at the Reinhardt Galleries, perhaps she would be looking for a position at one of the other ones. So I kept circulating myself about, always ending up nearby the Reinhardt Galleries. I observed the type of people who had appointments there. Rolex watches, alligator shoes, designer tote bags, and their noses way up in the air. There was really nothing at all trendy about them. They were welcomed into the Galleries based solely on the size of their wallets. I circled down to Canal Street and bought a fake Rolex and a fake Gucci backpack for ten and fifteen dollars, respectively. I also picked up a pair of trendy little rectangular sunglasses with purplish lenses from a street vendor. I was able to talk him down to three dollars. I needed to preserve some of my money for The Last Stand fund. I scanned a *New York Post* but found nothing about the splatter on West Broadway. I figured if anyone would cover it, the *Post* would; and with a full color spread. I headed back to the Reinhardt Galleries and watched from across the street. Then I saw two people approach who didn't fit the bill: a uniformed police officer and what appeared to be a plain-clothes detective. The detective had just finished smoking a cigarette. He extinguished it on the bottom of his shoe and flicked the dead butt into the street, about an inch from the curb. He and the uniformed cop entered the Reinhardt Galleries.

I counted to a hundred, then crossed the street, and conjured up the nerve to enter. I adopted a casual-yet-eccentric manner, and walked in. The place was sparsely furnished, and the walls were practically bare, except for an occasional modern art painting here and there. This was the reception and greeting area. The vast display of art was apparently behind closed doors in another part of the Galleries. The police were talking to an ultra-trendy at the reception desk, one that I hadn't yet had the displeasure of meeting. As I got closer I was able to overhear a snippet of conversation.

"I wasn't here, so you'd have to talk to them. Günther gets in around one o'clock or so, and Giselle usually saunters in anywhere between one-thirty and four-thirty, depending on where she spent the night."

The bratty receptionist caught sight of me, and the detective, obviously watching her eye movement, turned around to greet me.

"Is there a problem, officers?" I asked. I put on a slight British accent, an affectation that went over well in SoHo.

"May I help you?" the Brat cut in before either of them could answer.

"Teresa Traut is expecting me."

"Oh, um, did you have an appointment?" Flustered, she flipped through pages of a diary of some sort.

"She told me to come in any time this week after ten. Is she not here?"

"I'm very sorry, sir. Ms. Traut won't be in today. But I'd be happy to assist you."

The disguise was working. She thought I was some prize pigeon ready to shell out a fortune on glorified finger painting.

"Oh, what a bloody shame. I was so looking forward to finally meeting her in person."

There was an awkward pause. I looked at the

policemen, then to the Brat. "Oh pardon me. I seem to have interrupted. Perhaps I should come back a wee bit later?" I accidentally added a slight brogue to my accent. I hoped it would slip by undetected.

"Actually, since you're here, may I ask you a few questions?" the detective asked. "Just about art, if that's okay with you."

"Certainly."

"Did you ever hear of an artist named Dean Grimaldi?"

I thought. My brain started racing. The name was very familiar. I started to make a connection . . . I remembered seeing that name in the art listings section in the *Village Voice*. He was one of the artists whose work was being displayed down on Leonard Street—at a place called the TriBeCa Art Factory. I couldn't visualize the date, though.

"Wasn't he displaying at the T.A.F.?" I just used the initials. People who are full of shit use initials a lot.

"He showed some stuff there about six months ago, but not recently. Did you happen to see any of it?"

"No," I said. "He's not really my cup of tea."

The Brat gasped.

"Am I not entitled to an opinion?" I asked her, pretending to be insulted.

"It just so happens that he was a genius, and this world is a far sadder place without him," she said.

"I thought you said you'd never met him," the detective said to her.

"Well, never in person, but his art spoke to me."

"Excuse me, officer. What happened to Mister

Grimaldi?" I asked.

"He's dead. Run over by a tour bus yesterday afternoon."

"I'm so sorry. I didn't know."

Another awkward pause. The image of a double-decker bus filled with tourists was now imprinted on my mind, coupled with the horrible image of Dean Grimaldi's splatter on the street. I decided to break the ice this time. "Obviously, this is a bad time. I'll come back when Ms. Traut has returned."

"She's not coming back. It's her fault that Dean's dead," the Brat shouted at me.

"That's not true," the detective interrupted. "Ms. Traut had rejected Mr. Grimaldi's art work just prior to the accident," he explained to me. "We're just trying to figure out if it was a suicide or not." He turned back toward the Brat. "You better watch the things you say or you're gonna end up getting sued."

I thought it odd that the detective was so quick to jump to Teresa Traut's defense. He then returned his gruff gaze to me. He looked annoyed.

"I should be going now," I said, picking up on his vibe. "My condolences." Then I turned around and walked out without looking back.

It was now 11:30 a.m. so I stuffed the sunglasses and fake Rolex into the fake Gucci bag and high-tailed it over to The Last Stand. I needed to talk to Zane. When I got there, Vincent was getting ready to open the doors to the general public. Zane, the pre-patron, was sitting at the bar, transfixed by a "Gilligan's Island" marathon. I was going to have some major competition for Zane's attention.

"What are you doing here so early?" Vincent asked. "Playing hooky?"

"For the whole week," I answered.

"I better order some extra kegs."

"Gilligan!" shouted the Skipper. Zane howled.

"Hey, Zane. How's it going?" I said.

"Why do they always give Gilligan the most important job every episode? He's only gonna screw it up."

I decided to drop the bombshell on Zane.

"Do you know an artist named Dean Grimaldi?"

"He's dead," Zane answered, not even switching his focus from the television.

"You knew this already?"

"Sure. Ran in front of a tour bus yesterday after his art work was rejected."

"Geez," Vincent said. "That must've been a pretty uncomfortable moment for the tour guide."

I felt like a total and complete imbecile. Zane had all the information; I hadn't needed to masquerade around in a knock-off Rolex and faux Gucci gear. If Zane knew this much, it was likely he knew even more; maybe he'd learned some new details about Teresa Traut.

"How much stuff did Mr. and Mrs. Howell bring for a three-hour tour?" Zane asked. "It's as if they knew they were gonna be shipwrecked."

I was losing the battle for Zane's attention.

"Yeah," Vincent chimed in. "And how come the Professor can build a car out of trees and coconuts, but he can't fix the damn boat?"

Vincent wasn't helping any. I figured I'd go with the

flow.

"Maybe it was all a big conspiracy. How long after the Kennedy assassination did this so-called shipwreck occur?"

Silence. That shut 'em up long enough to introduce the subject of Teresa Traut.

"Speaking of conspiracy theories, you think Teresa Traut had anything to do with the death of Dean Grimaldi yesterday?"

"Are you sure he's dead?" Zane said.

"His guts were all over the street."

"Are you sure they were *his* guts?"

"Zane, are you suggesting that Teresa Traut and Dean Grimaldi planted somebody else's guts at the scene of the accident?"

"I can't believe you're having this conversation without any alcohol, Harry," Vincent said, and then mercifully placed a pint in front of me.

"Did you ever see that Lucy episode?" Zane continued.

It was hopeless. I accepted my defeat and engaged Zane in sitcom talk.

"Which episode would that be, Zane?"

"It was either 'Here's Lucy' or 'The Lucy Show'—I forget which—but Danny Thomas is this painter . . ."

"The 'Make Room for Daddy' guy?" Vincent asked.

"Yeah. That guy. And they fake his death to increase the value of his art."

"What was Lucy's cut?"

"Don't really know. They didn't go into it."

"How'd Danny Thomas collect, if he was supposed to

be dead?"

"He disguised himself as his twin brother. Put on a fake mustache or something."

I couldn't believe it. Zane and Vincent's idiotic discussion actually gave me an idea. And a way to meet Teresa Traut.

"Can I use your phone?"

I dialed the number that I had memorized earlier that morning. An answering machine picked up with a computer-automated voice: "Please leave a mes-sage." What to do? Maybe this wasn't her number. Perhaps she was unlisted. Perhaps she didn't live in Manhattan. Perhaps she was listed under a different name. But perhaps this was the right number. What could I lose?

"Hello, Ms. Traut. This is Harrison Spangler of Last Stand Management. I understand you've recently moved on from Reinhardt. I have a wonderful opportunity here that I think you'd be perfect for—a very promising artist whose work is exclusively owned by us. I think the value will be sky-rocketing in the very near future."

I left the phone number of the bar and hung up.

"What're you up to?" Vincent asked.

"Another typical hare-brained scheme."

I surveyed the three paintings scattered around the bar. I looked over at Zane. His focus had once again returned to the TV.

"You know," he said, "now that I think about it, maybe Ginger was really Marilyn Monroe and they faked her death, too."

TWO HOURS LATER, the phone rang. It was Thomas Traut calling to tell me that I had the wrong number. Apparently he got calls for Teresa all the time, but had no idea who she was. I thanked him and told him I was sorry that I disturbed him. After I hung up, I concentrated on the image in the phone book. Just above T Traut was Ronald Traut. I read the associated phone number in the image and dialed it. A woman answered.

"Yes?"

"Teresa Traut?"

"Maybe. Depends who this is."

"Harrison Spangler of Last Stand Management."

"Never heard of you. Teresa's not in. May I take a message?"

"Sure. Ask her if she'd like to get in on the ground floor of an exclusively owned artist."

"You can't own an artist, just his or her work."

"Really?"

"Well . . . legally speaking. Where did you say you were calling from?"

"Last Stand Management."

"You'd better let the phone company know that they're listing your number as 'Last Stand Tavern' on Caller ID."

"But it's all one. A tavern, a gallery and a place where an artist can feel at home while signing everything over to you."

"You're not very subtle, which saves time I suppose. But I'm not in that end of the business. I appraise art. I have as little to do with the artist as possible."

"Apparently you're not in *any* end of the business

right now." There was silence at the other end.

"Look," I said. "Dean Grimaldi was a hack—you know that and I know that. But now that he's dead, his art is going to sell for a lot of money, and you're going to look like a fool. I'm offering you a way to get back at Günther and Giselle."

After a short pause she finally spoke. "Okay, what's the deal?"

CHAPTER THREE

AFTER REVEALING THE KEY POINTS of my hare-brained scheme to her, Teresa Traut agreed to meet me at The Last Stand at ten o'clock the following morning to take a look at Zane's art. I needed to talk Vincent into opening early. It was easy. I just told him that I wanted to use the bar for illegal activity and that I needed him to head it up. He was as excited as a malevolent kid with a bat in a Hummel factory. I stayed up with Zane all night making him paint. I wanted more than three pieces for Teresa.

"What else can you tell me about Teresa Traut, Zane?"

Zane didn't hear me. He was stoned and painting—it was even harder to gain his attention than if a "Brady Bunch" episode were on. His cat kept rubbing up against him, and Zane would absentmindedly pet her. The cat's fur would shed and become airborne whenever he did. Half the time, the cat's hair found its way onto the canvas, and would attach itself to the wet paint. It gave it a rather interesting texture. Zane kept right on without even noticing. He was doing the two things he loved most: painting and getting high. Or should I say, getting high and painting. The chronology of these events was very important. Zane wouldn't even look at the canvas until he was pleasantly buzzed. One would think that since Zane got stoned every day, he'd be rather prolific and have a large collection of finished works. However, once he got stoned, he'd forget that he was planning to paint and would end up playing with a shoelace and laughing uncontrollably whenever the cat swatted at it.

An hour later, Zane spoke. "She's gonna hate this, Harry. I just know she is."

"It doesn't matter what she thinks. She's gonna go for the pitch and you're gonna reap the rewards."

"It matters to me. Getting the Traut seal of approval means a lot."

"Why?"

"If she likes it, you're golden. You can hang your stuff anywhere. If she says she doesn't like it, nobody'll show it."

"If she's so influential, why did Reinhardt let her go?"

"They've been waiting for an excuse. Everybody in the art world hates her guts. They think she has too much power. 'Curatorial fascism' they call it."

"So now that Dean Grimaldi's work increased in value, they were able to discredit her?" I asked.

"Yeah. Seems like she was set up, doesn't it?"

Zane paused. His last statement triggered the conspiracy theory gears in his cannabis-clouded little head.

"Do you think that Reinhardt . . ."

"Just keep painting, Zane."

By three in the morning, Zane had painted three more pieces. They were abstract moderns, so no one would know how much time and thought he actually put into them. I called it a night, went home and tried to get some sleep, but to no avail. I talked over my strategy with Julia. Yup, it was another typical hare-brained scheme, befitting a 175 I.Q. no doubt.

When ten a.m. rolled around, I was eagerly waiting at The Last Stand, with Zane's new pieces hanging. Vincent and Zane were both sipping coffee, trying to cast off their fatigue. Twenty-five minutes later, Teresa Traut stepped through the door. Fashionably late and fashionably attired. She looked at Vincent, then at Zane, and then finally at me.

"Harrison Spangler, I presume?" she asked.

She exuded a very tough exterior; not unlike Julia.

"That would be me," I answered. I stood up and extended my hand, which she ignored.

"Is this the . . . art?" she asked in an ever-so-sarcastic tone.

"And the artist as well." I moved over to Zane and introduced them before Teresa said anything too disparaging in front of him.

Teresa walked around the bar and looked at each of the works. She leaned in to get a closer look at one and then sneezed.

"Is there a cat in here? I'm deathly allergic to cats."

She sneezed again. I bit my lip. She sneezed a third time. I bit harder, nearly drawing blood. Thus far the morning couldn't have gone any worse.

"Why don't you have a seat at the bar and have a cup of coffee? Get your adrenaline up and maybe the sneezing will pass."

Vincent went behind the bar and poured her a cup. "Milk? Sugar?" he asked.

"When was it brewed?" she asked.

"About an hour ago."

"And you expect me to drink it?"

I was mistaken. Apparently it could have gone worse.

"We'll make a fresh pot," I interjected.

"All right. I prefer a dark roast, and make sure to grind the beans finely."

Vincent picked up an industrial-sized can of Chock Full O' Nuts and slid it across the bar to Teresa.

"This is what I got. If you want the gourmet shit, go outside to one of them fancy SoHo bee-stros, and get it yourself."

Teresa didn't say a word. Instead she began sneezing again.

"Maybe Zane would like to get one for you," I said. I shooed Zane out and gave him a twenty dollar bill, hoping that would be enough to cover a cup of designer coffee. I quickly moved toward Teresa to try to keep her from walking out. But when her sneezing subsided, she looked at Vincent and smiled.

"Just give me what's left in the pot," she said. "Black is fine."

She and Vincent exchanged glances.

"You've got good people here, Spangler," Teresa said. "I hate spineless gallery owners. This guy'll do just fine. Now let's get down to business before little Andy Warhol gets back."

She looked at the paintings again. "The art isn't horrible. But we'll need an additional marketing angle for it, if it's going to work. A dead artist only gets you so far."

"Missing and presumed dead," I corrected her. "That adds an element of intrigue."

"Whatever. Still not enough. Especially on the heels of Dean Gri-." She sneezed again. "Are you sure there are no cats in here?"

It was time to come clean. "Actually," I said, "it's embedded in the paintings. Zane has a cat that sheds a lot and the fur makes its way onto the canvases."

"That's our angle!" She practically burst. "The cat is his collaborator! What's the cat's name?"

"Um, Mittens."

"That's gotta change. Maybe something Spanish-sounding. Like Reynaldo, or Francisco."

"The cat's female."

"Doesn't matter."

"I like this chick, Harry," Vincent said. "She's smarter than you are!"

"Now let's talk about your side, Mr. Spangler. How do you handle the artist's . . . disappearance?"

"I think the less you know about it, the better," I said. "The police will undoubtedly ask questions—especially after the Grimaldi incident—and I don't think you should even have a clue as to the specifics."

"I agree," she said, "but I need to know the big picture before I sign on."

"Basically, Vincent and I will arrange for Zane's disappearance. We'll leave clues for the police to lead them the wrong way. Meanwhile, Zane will be on a bus headed far away. All cash transactions, of course. He'll make contact every month or so, and arrange to send us any new pieces that he's finished that we can sell to Reinhardt as newly discovered works. If the police start suspecting us as murderers—which they won't—Zane will return. Just a spacey, stoned-out artist who went away without telling anybody. No murder charges will be filed, and Reinhardt Galleries will have a huge display of grossly over-valued art work."

"What about the cat?"

"The cat will go with him. Zane wouldn't go anywhere without her."

"Just make sure to shave the cat and keep some of the fur here with us. We'll need it for the new paintings to be authenticated."

Vincent was right. She was smarter than I was. Another Julia-esque similarity. Then she continued her shameless flirting with Vincent. Would the similarities never end?

Zane returned fifteen minutes later with Teresa's designer coffee. She played him like a pro. She told him that his work had loads of potential, and then they spoke of textures and colors and nuances. Zane was putty in her hands. He had received the Traut seal of approval. Nothing else in the world mattered to him.

So now Teresa had cozied up to everyone but me. It was as if she already knew that I was hooked, so she needn't bother. At least Julia used to acknowledge my neediness before she'd unleash some crushing mental anguish upon me en route to my emotional destruction. Did I really want to go down this road again? I stared at Teresa. She didn't notice, since she was too preoccupied with Vincent and Zane fawning all over her. I looked closely at her eyes: the way she batted them when she laughed, the way she widened them when she listened, and the way she shot bullets with them when she noticed I was staring at her. I quickly moved my gaze to the television, which didn't work out too well, because now I was pretending to look thoughtfully at a commercial for erectile dysfunction. I quickly excused myself and headed toward the rest room. I needed to regroup.

After giving myself a quick pep talk in the cracked bathroom mirror, I emerged from the rest room. Zane was sipping a late-morning beer and laughing at "My Three Sons." Even stranger, Vincent was sipping a late-morning beer and laughing at "My Three Sons." And disturbingly, Teresa Traut was nowhere to be found.

"Is Teresa in the ladies' room?" I asked.

"Nah," said Vincent. "She left. Told me to tell you goodbye for her."

"Goodbye?"

"Yeah."

"Anything else?"

"She said she'd probably call here later. She may even stop by after hours, if you know what I mean." Vincent licked his lips lasciviously.

"Thanks for pulling this off for me, Harry," Zane added during a commercial. "I think this experience is gonna change my life."

Zane didn't know how right he was.

CHAPTER FOUR

I PLANTED MYSELF across the street from the West 54th Street brownstone where, according to the Manhattan telephone directory, one Ronald Traut was living. I had gone from intrigued passerby to obsessed stalker in just a couple of days; and by month's end, if all went according to plan, assorted felonies would be committed.

I never pegged Teresa as a Hell's Kitchen denizen. Perhaps that's where Ronald Traut, whoever he may be, came into the picture. The detective that I saw at the Reinhardt Galleries was standing in front of the building with the uniformed cop, each smoking a cigarette. The detective savored a final rushed drag, and extinguished the butt beneath his foot. The uniform still had more than half his cigarette to go, but dutifully dropped it to the ground, stomped out the embers and obediently followed. The detective walked up to the front door, perused the buzzers and pressed one. He waited for a moment and then was buzzed in. He and his uniformed sidekick disappeared into the brownstone.

Was Teresa ratting us out? I had thought she went along with the plan a little too easily. Was she cutting a deal with the cops? Perhaps she was more involved in the

Grimaldi death than I thought.

My hands shook. I popped into a deli on the corner and bought an overpriced can of beer. I drank it out of a paper bag, and it seemed to steel my nerves a bit. I returned to my surveillance position across the street from Teresa's brownstone. Half an hour later, the uniformed cop left the building . . . alone. Another thirty minutes went by before I saw the detective walk out. He lit up a cigarette as he came out and then went merrily on his way. What the hell was going on up there? Initially, my plan was to wait for Teresa to show up and "accidentally" bump into her. Just some harmless stalking. But now . . . things weren't as they appeared, that was certain. I needed to find Zane and see if his art world contacts could help connect the dots.

I hopped the R train down to Prince Street and headed over to The Last Stand. No sign of Zane or Vincent. Tucker, the relief bartender that hated me, was in charge.

"Tucker, have you seen Zane?"

Tucker was a smug bastard and he had a smug expression on his face. He just stood there, as if he were trying to think of something smug to say, but couldn't so he settled on just looking smug instead. Five seconds went by before he finally spoke: "Hiya, Harry. Whaddya drinking?"

"Where's Vincent?"

Another five seconds went by as he screwed up his face before coming up with: "That's a drink I've never heard of, a *Wheres Vincent*. What's it made with?" He chuckled at his retarded little joke. And he chuckled smugly.

Tucker was an actor/improv comic. Problem was he had no talent and he wasn't the least bit clever. But he didn't let those little shortcomings stand in his way. He'd regularly rent out a small theatre and invite everyone he knew to pay him twelve dollars to sit through an evening of torture. It was great fun hearing what each of his friends would say to him after the show. "Really interesting stuff" or "It's good to see you working"— euphemistic expressions that mean "you suck and you should give it up, but I'm too polite to tell you so."

"Can I see some I.D., young man?" Tucker continued. "I can't serve you any *Wheres Vincents* unless you're of age." More self-satisfied chuckling ensued. I felt like strangling the smug retard. Inexplicably, I ordered a beer instead and plopped myself down onto my barstool. Tucker placed a pint of all foam in front of me. I leaned over the bar, dumped it out and poured myself a proper pint with a respectable half inch head on it. Tucker didn't care. He was probably trying to think of another *Wheres Vincent* joke to use.

I stared at one of Zane's paintings. The cat hairs embedded in it formed an almost symmetrical swirl. Very captivating; almost hypnotic. If it had actually been planned one might call it "genius." And of course that was exactly what Teresa was going to do. Genius collaboration between human and feline to create trans-species art. Danny Thomas and Lucy never could have come up with that twist. I finished my pint.

"Can I get you another *Wheres Vincent*, Harry?" Tucker interrupted my train of thought.

"No, Tucker. I'd like a 'Tell me where the fuck

Vincent is before I kick your ass.' Do you know how to make that, or should I show you?" Unfortunately, I only thought that response. My actual reply was "Please, Tucker, tell me where Vincent is."

"He went somewhere with Zane."

"Where?"

"I dunno. You want another beer?"

"That's okay. I'll help myself." I leaned over the bar and poured myself another pint. I figured I'd wait for Vincent and Zane to return and the drunker I was, the easier it would be to block out Tucker. Four pints later, my co-conspirators still hadn't surfaced. I threw down a more-than-generous tip for Tucker and asked him to tell Vincent and Zane that I was looking for them and would be back. He made some inane joke, but thankfully I was too drunk to comprehend it.

I staggered around SoHo for a while. School had just let out for the day and I saw a few of my students pointing at me from across the street and laughing. I took a mental snapshot of their faces for future reference. I passed by the Reinhardt Galleries a few times. No activity to speak of. Maybe the ultra-trendies were taking the afternoon off. I grabbed a cup of designer coffee from a trendy little bistro to combat some of my drunkenness and headed back to The Last Stand. When I got there, Teresa was sitting at the bar, engaged in lively conversation with Tucker. I quickly popped a breath mint and chased it with some hot coffee, nearly burning off my soft palate in the process. I sat down next to Teresa.

"Fancy meeting you here," I said, hating myself as the words came out of my mouth. What a totally stupid and cliché thing to say. Luckily, she had been talking to Tucker this whole time, so my phrasing was brilliant and original in comparison.

"I was hoping you'd be here," Teresa said, holding up her martini glass. "Thank goodness you showed up now; if this guy asked me if I wanted another *Is Harrison Spangler here*, I might have hung myself."

"I know what you mean," I said. "I've had my share of *Wheres Vincents*."

She smiled. A genuine smile. And it came from something that I said. And she came in here looking for me, not for Vincent. Maybe my luck was finally changing. She spoke again.

"Is there somewhere we can go to talk? I don't want Zane or Vincent to hear any of this."

TEN MINUTES LATER we were in front of my decrepit walkup tenement building on Eldridge Street. Punctured, smelly garbage bags greeted us as I pushed open the broken "security" door and we entered into the vestibule. We climbed the three flights of stairs without encountering a single junkie or drag queen—a rarity. I opened the door to my apartment.

Since I wasn't expecting any visitors, the place was a mess. Hopefully she'd see me as an eccentric rather than a slob. I went into the kitchen to fetch beverages. By the time I returned with our cocktails, Teresa had already cleared off a spot on the couch and sat down.

"Um, I know he's your friend and all," she said, "but that Tucker guy can't be anywhere near the place during the art exhibit."

"He's not my friend. That guy hates my guts."

"If you say so. But all he talked about was you and how smart you are."

"Pardon the expression, but he was just blowing smoke up your ass." Yikes! Did I actually just say that to Teresa?

"Nonetheless," she continued, unfazed by my vulgar non-witticism, "he really can't be there. He'll sour the critics against us."

"Agreed," I said. "Anything else?"

"Yes," she said, "I was thinking . . ."

There it was. The three scariest words in the English language: *I was thinking*—a euphemism for *the next thing I'm going to say will totally piss you off and go against everything you've already carefully planned out.*

"The cat has to stay," she said.

"Why?"

"Think about it. The plan doesn't make sense. If the cat is missing, they won't think that Zane is dead; just that he left and took the cat with him. Just another flaky artist."

"We'll leave the door to his apartment open as well as the windows. The cat will appear to have just run away under those circumstances."

"But if the cat is still here, they'd be more likely to believe that Zane's dead. He would never go anywhere without that cat, right?"

She had a valid point. But getting Zane to agree to it was another matter.

"And also," she continued, "if we have the cat in our

possession, we can launch some solo shows while we wait for the new pieces."

"Solo shows? For the cat?"

"Günther and Giselle were in the process of making a deal for Siamese elephant art before I left. And Siamese elephant art is not paintings *of* Siamese elephants, but paintings *by* Siamese elephants."

"So we're gonna launch the cat's solo efforts, and when the 'long lost collaborative masterpieces' come in, they'll discuss how the cat has progressed as an artist?"

"Now you're starting to understand the art world."

"The only problem is, Zane won't leave that cat behind," I said.

"He will if it's the only way he'll become a successful artist."

"I'm not so sure."

"I am," she said. "Artists are all the same. Trust me on that. They'd sell their mothers into slavery to get their work shown. And besides, I'm sure you could convince him, Harrison."

Harrison. She called me *Harrison.* I looked over at Julia's urn.

"All right, I'll talk to Zane."

She smiled. She knew she had me under her thumb. And she was right. It didn't matter one iota that I had seen two cops leaving her building earlier today. It made no difference that she was living in an apartment belonging to some guy named Ronald, and that maybe she was about to play me the way she was playing him.

She raised her cocktail and toasted: "To art."

The art of deception, I thought. I drank anyway.

"Who's Ronald Traut?" I blurted out. I couldn't contain myself.

"He's my brother, not that it's any of your business."

"You live with him?"

"Of course not. He got married and moved to Oswego. So I got his rent-controlled apartment."

That explained the Ronald Traut dilemma. Now what about the cops at her apartment? I gingerly prodded my way into the topic.

"Any word on the Grimaldi investigation?"

"Investigation?" she said, taken aback. "What's there to investigate?"

"Whether it was an accident or a suicide, I guess."

She sat on the couch practically devoid of emotion.

"They came to my apartment today," she said in a dull monotone.

"Who?" I played dumb, not wanting to alert her to my stalking behavior.

"The cops," she said. "They determined that it wasn't an accident." And then a single teardrop formed at the corner of her left eye. It slowly made its way down her cheek. I sat down next to her. Keeping one eye on Julia's urn, I placed my hand on her shoulder.

"It wasn't your fault, you know. People don't just commit suicide over one little rejection. Sure, it may have been a last straw, but that last straw was going to come sooner or later." I gently rubbed her shoulder.

"Could you get me a tissue, please?"

"Of course," I said rising from the couch. "Where are my manners?" I didn't have any tissues, so I gave her a roll of toilet paper instead.

"The cops were pretty nice," she continued. She pulled a sheet from the roll and eradicated the tear from her otherwise expressionless face. "One of them actually asked me out."

"What? Is that appropriate?"

"He's very sweet."

"So, what did you say?"

"I told him I was very busy working with a new artist and planning his first exhibit."

I felt relieved, but only for a moment.

"He was still persistent, though," she continued, "so I invited him to the opening of Zane's show."

All I could hear in my head was Ricky Ricardo screaming: "Lucy!!!!! You've got a lot of 'splaining to do!!!"

And 'splain she did.

"I was thinking . . ." she began.

CHAPTER FIVE

"NO FUCKING WAY, HARRY," Zane said, clutching the cat and pulling her close against his chest. "Mittens comes with me or I don't go at all."

My head was killing me. I had been balancing a deadly combination of beer, liquor and caffeine in my system and it was being thrown off kilter by the contact high I was getting from the cloud of cannabis in Zane's apartment. Even the cat looked stoned; or should I say, she looked more stoned than usual.

"Okay, Zane," I said, using a little teacher trick. "You tell me how you want to do it. How are you going to take the cat with you?"

"I put her in her little crate and we go."

"On a bus?"

"Yeah."

"To Mexico?"

"Yeah."

"How will she eat and shit?"

"The same way she always does."

"Let me re-phrase that. *Where* will she eat and shit?"

He didn't have a quick answer for that one. I used the opening to pound my point home. "If the police are searching for you, they're going to check the airports, the train stations and the bus stations. If you're traveling with a screaming cat in a box, you're going to be a lot more memorable, and therefore more easily identifiable."

Zane became very thoughtful all of a sudden.

"She's putting you up to this, isn't she?"

"What are you talking about?"

"Teresa Traut. You have to watch out for her, Harry."

"I'm watching out for all of us, Zane." A cliché response, to say the least, but after all, it was Zane I was talking to. He thrived upon the cliché and the familiar, and that particular line had been used in many a sitcom. But Zane definitely had a point. Teresa needed to be watched. And not just in a stalking sense. Her extending an invitation to a police detective to join us at our actual crime scene was not the swiftest move; at least not on the surface. But she explained that having a detective on the scene when Zane didn't show up to his own show would help fuel the story, and the journalists would be able to go to town on that. Also, she reasoned, having a cop on her side and in her favor was better than not having one at all. By blowing him off and refusing his advances, she'd run the risk of creating an enemy in the police department. Much as I wanted to disagree with her, I couldn't. Her logic wasn't flawed; provided that the plan went off without a hitch. And that included the damn cat staying.

"Maybe we should just call the whole thing off," Zane said.

"It's up to you, Zane," I said. "After all, it's your art work we're showing."

I remembered what Teresa had said about artists all

being the same; that they'd sell their mothers into slavery to show a painting. I hoped that Zane would prove her wrong. Then I could use Zane's refusal to gracefully extricate myself from this mess that was quickly spiraling out of control. But Zane caved.

"You'll take good care of Mittens?" he asked me.

"Of course, Zane."

"Promise me."

I hated making a promise if I didn't know that I could keep it. I had come up short too many times in the past. I drew a deep breath and exhaled.

"I promise," I said. Zane then proceeded to show me the cat's toys, food, catnip, and litter. He told me all of the cat's likes, dislikes, and peculiarities. I learned more about Mittens's hairball history than I ever needed to know.

It was strange: Zane didn't care a whit about leaving New York and letting his friends and family think he was missing and presumed dead, but leaving the cat was a trauma. Maybe it's because Mittens never told him to get a real job and make something of himself. Zane hadn't spoken to his mother in two years, after she refused to continue sending him money from Minnesota to support his art habit. The cat was nonjudgmental and didn't care that Zane had no bank account, no credit cards, no driver's license, and no job. And these same qualities made him the perfect person to pull off the hare-brained caper.

Zane accepted the situation by firing up his bong and taking a few hits. I placed a fresh canvas on his easel and put a paintbrush in his hand. He moved the paintbrush around in some sort of ritualistic manner, but nowhere near the canvas; almost as if he were "air painting." Then Mittens pounced on it. Zane giggled, dropped the brush, lifted the cat and gave her tender kisses on the head.

"Daddy won't be gone too long, my wittle pwincess," he whispered to the cat in a sickening baby-talk tone. "And Uncle Harry pwomised me that he'll take good care of you. Yes, he will."

Then Zane put the cat down and started painting.

* * *

FOR IMMEDIATE RELEASE

LAST STAND GALLERIES TO PREMIERE CONFLUENCE OF HERBIVORE AND CARNIVORE ART

New York, NY—The newly refurbished Last Stand Galleries (LSG) is pleased to announce the premiere of "CATHARSIS," the joint effort by abstract expressionist artist Zane Burroughs and his tiger cat, Aldonza.

The paintings, informed by personal and universal myth, represent their passion, angst and whimsy. They incorporate issues of confrontation, self-realization and empowerment in human and feline voices on a journey of discovery. The tension between dark and light is vibrantly played out in such works as: "Guzzling Wretches & the 2-faced gerbil trapped inside a fish bowl of primordial ooze"; "Snot on the cyclone"; "I'm not feeling Soft & fuzzy today"; and the newly created "Brunching with my demons."

Zane Burroughs, an avowed herbivore, was born in Minnesota, but has lived in New York City for the last four years. He is self-taught in drawing and painting and works in an expressionistic style with multimedia on canvas. This exhibition is a strong illustration of his statement, "My works are a portrait of a spiritual and emotional journey, representing closures, and new openings in my life, as well as a testament to the herbs that sustain me."

Aldonza, an unrepentant carnivore, is approximately four years old and has the uncanny ability to express herself on canvas not just with her paws, but with a full body approach.

The exhibition is on view from May 18th through June 12th.

The Opening Reception will be held on Monday, May 17th from 7 to 9 PM, followed by a curatorial talk by Teresa Traut.

Mr. Burroughs and Ms. Aldonza will be available for panel discussions and interviews.

LSG is located on Spring Street (between Mulberry and Lafayette Streets).

* * *

TERESA WAS RUNNING a well-oiled publicity machine. She had a healthy disdain for the truth, which helped her a great deal. Zane never saw the press release. Teresa never even consulted with him about it. She concocted his quote and the titles of the paintings while playing word association games during a four-martini lunch.

The next few weeks flew by. Teresa worked her contacts in the press and in the assorted sordid galleries. Zane and Mittens/Aldonza completed a few more paintings. Vincent and Tucker worked on getting the bar converted into a trendy art gallery. They took the path of least resistance and opted to go for the "dive" look. Based upon the premise that it's hip to be in controlled faux filth, the crappier the place looked the better. Of course, unbeknownst to the ultra-trendies, they were going to be in unbridled real filth. So the bulk of the work came in hanging the new paintings and focusing lights on them. Teresa dropped by often, either to supervise the "renovation" or to add her input as to where the paintings should hang and how they should be grouped. I returned to substitute teaching and stopped by the bar/gallery shortly after three o'clock every afternoon to help out. It was great seeing Teresa almost every day. It seemed as if she would make sure to be there around three o'clock, just so she could see me. Or perhaps I was imagining it. Either way, it made me happy. And there was now no need for me to wait outside her apartment hoping to "accidentally" bump into her.

MONDAY, MAY 17TH finally arrived. I arose at nine a.m. after a mostly sleepless night. It had been three days since my last drink. Not a moral decision, mind you; I just didn't have enough time. I threw some coffee grinds into the coffee maker, and while I waited for it to brew, I picked up Julia's urn and cradled it in my arms. I could feel her disapproval. I wasn't exactly fulfilling my potential, was I?

Over the weekend I had gone shopping in Chinatown, where I purchased a rolling travel bag, clothing, assorted toiletries, an English-Spanish dictionary, a portable CD-player, loads of double-A batteries, and ten of Zane's favorite CDs. All cash transactions from vendors who spoke little or no English. Earlier that week I took the PATH train to Newark and bought a one-way Greyhound bus ticket to Tulsa from a slack-jawed, gum-cracking ticket agent; a cash payment with a seemingly brain-dead human element involved, thus no record and no reliable witness. According to the plan, once Zane reached Tulsa, he'd take a Jefferson Lines bus to El Paso, and from there he could just walk across the border into Juarez. The whole trip would take about three days. And Zane was actually excited about it. He was off to live the artist's life in the land of marijuana and Galavision.

I placed the judgmental urn back on the shelf and returned to the kitchen to watch the coffee drip, trying to will it to brew more quickly. It looked like wax dripping off a black candle. Coffee that you could eat with a fork. I was going to need it.

The opening was slated to begin at seven o'clock that evening. I needed to be at The Last Stand by six at the latest to meet the caterers. That left me nine hours to: (1) arrange a disappearance, (2) leave clues to throw the police off, and (3) bring the cat to the groomer. Since Teresa was so allergic, I had to take on all cat-related duties.

After chewing on some coffee, I packed up Zane's

rolling travel bag and headed over to The Last Stand. I set up a litter pan, food and water dishes, a scratching post and an assortment of toys in the back room for the Great Aldonza's amusement during the show. I left the travel bag in there as well. I'd come back for it later.

Next it was off to Zane's apartment. I rang his buzzer for about ten minutes before he answered. Zane had overslept, which wasn't much of a shock; in fact, I had budgeted our time for that particular event, so we were still right on schedule. Zane made some coffee, and had a joint while he waited for it to brew. I didn't interrupt him. The more he went through his usual morning routine, the better.

"I wish I could be there, Harry."

"The opening?" I asked.

"Yeah. It's been such a dream of mine and now . . ."

"I'll take lots of pictures."

"Thanks. Not the same, though."

"I know," I said. Then a stroke of brilliance. "What would you have worn tonight?"

"Oh, I've had that planned for years," Zane said.

"Show me."

Zane went into his closet and pulled out a shirt that was so ugly it would be considered trendy.

"Try it on," I said.

Zane shrugged and put the shirt on. Still ugly, but he was able to pull it off fashion-wise. He made it look retro-ugly.

I had Zane lay out his entire "dream outfit" as if he were readying himself for the show. A nice touch. What conclusions would the police draw when they found this in the apartment?

Zane owned two identical "Ren and Stimpy" t-shirts. He ended up buying two by accident because he was high at the time of the purchase. I had him put one on and walk around the apartment in it for awhile. Then I told him to take it off and place it in a black garbage bag. After doing so I had him put on the second t-shirt.

"You wear this shirt the rest of the day, you understand? Don't wear a jacket outside. Make sure your neighbors see you."

"Okay, Harry."

There was an awkward silence. Zane looked at Mittens.

"I guess you should start saying your goodbyes," I said.

"Do you have to take her now?"

"We've got a grooming appointment. I also want to get her acclimated to the bar as early as possible today. It'll be better for her."

Zane lifted Mittens and covered her with kisses.

"Danny Thomas didn't have to say goodbye to his loved ones; he just pretended to be his own twin brother and collected the money," he said.

"That was a sitcom, Zane. It couldn't be further from real life."

"Yeah, I know. That's what scares me."

He looked into Mittens's eyes and gave her a final kiss right on the nose.

"Daddy loves you very much, and he'll be back soon."

Then Zane placed her into her crate and handed the

crate to me.

"Take good care of her, or I will hunt you down and kill you," Zane said. And he was dead serious.

"I'll take good care of her, Zane."

I shook his hand, and reassured him some more.

"Why don't you go ask one of your neighbors to come to the opening tonight?"

Zane nodded in agreement.

"Good idea, Harry. You're always scheming, aren't you?"

I smiled as if Zane were making a joke, trying to hide the fact that his words were ripping me apart. I grabbed a Japanese baseball cap that was hanging on the back of the door, and placed it on Zane's head.

"I'll see you in front of the PATH station in two hours," I said, grabbing the black garbage bag with my free hand. "And don't take off that hat."

I LIED TO ZANE about wanting to get Mittens acclimated to the bar. The real reason that I needed her so early was because she wasn't just getting groomed, she was getting a complete makeover. Teresa arranged a visit with a cat groomer in the West Village and Mittens needed a sedative before the work could begin. I felt guilty when I dropped her off. I'd broken my promise to Zane within only minutes of taking his cat into my custody; but I just couldn't say "no" to Teresa. I headed over to The Last Stand. It was time to fall off the three-day wagon.

When I arrived, my regular barstool was occupied by a tough-looking bald guy wearing a shiny sweat suit accessorized with lots of gold jewelry. I looked over to

Vincent, who refused to make eye contact with me. He was too busy fawning all over the new customer. I sat down at the empty stool next to him and extended my hand.

"Harry," I said.

The stranger looked at my hand as if it were a turd, and then looked over to Vincent.

"Something's trying to touch me, Vinny," he said. "Could you take care of this?"

Vincent quickly inserted himself between us and gently pushed me toward the other end of the bar. He poured me a quick shot.

"Harry," he said, "that's my Uncle Sal. He just got out of the joint last week."

A bead of sweat ran down the side of my face.

"He's not staying for the show, is he? We've got a cop on the guest list."

"Don't worry. He won't stay long."

"Hey Vinny," Uncle Sal called out. "Quit talking to that asshole and pour me another drink."

"Maybe you should go, Harry. Let me take care of this."

Vincent poured me a shot of bourbon for the road and assured me that Uncle Sal would be gone before the show began. I downed the shot, grabbed the rolling bag from the back room, and hurried out.

"Hey, Pete!" I heard from across the street. The Nasty Drunk was ambling across Spring Street and staggering toward The Last Stand. I could only imagine what Uncle Sal was going to do to him.

I steeled my resolve with a few more empty-stomach

whiskeys at an old-time Village bar on University Place. It was conveniently located a few blocks from the 9th Street PATH station, which was where I was meeting Zane. I tried to put Uncle Sal out of my mind, but it was to no avail. He just gave me a bad feeling all over. I hoped Vincent would be able to get rid of him soon. It also bothered me that Sal was sitting on my barstool. I felt violated. I downed another whiskey.

The rolling bag, black garbage bag and I made it to the PATH station right on time. Zane was late, of course. His bus was scheduled to leave in ninety minutes. It would take only forty minutes to get to Newark, so I wasn't worried . . . yet.

I went over the plan while I waited. I needed to drop off Zane's clothes with Vincent, pick up the cat from the groomer, get myself dressed, and direct the caterers to set up the buffet tables. Then sit back and wait for the people to arrive. Teresa will give her talk, seem mildly concerned that Zane is late to his own opening and then introduce the cat. When Zane doesn't show up at all, we'll go to his apartment and discover he's missing and foul play is suspected. The press will have a field day, the value will go up, and Teresa will be grateful for having met me. She'll fall into my arms and we'll live happily ever after. That was the plan, complete with Hollywood-style ending. But first, I had to get Zane onto a bus and Zane was M.I.A. at the moment.

I checked the front zippered compartment of the bag for the fiftieth time to make sure the bus ticket was still there, and for the fiftieth time, it was. Just another one of my endearing obsessive-compulsive traits. Zane arrived ten minutes later, although the wait seemed like hours. Even though it was a brisk fifty-five degrees, I was sweating quite a bit. We descended into the station, paid our fares and pushed through the turnstiles. We stood next to each other on the platform but didn't speak. Not until the Newark-bound train arrived. I handed off the rolling bag to Zane.

"Ticket is in the front compartment," I said.

"Thanks," Zane said with a quick nod of his head. I pulled the Japanese baseball cap off his head and put it into the black garbage bag alongside the "Ren and Stimpy" t-shirt.

"Just another item to remember you by," I said.

Zane half-smiled at me. "My downstairs neighbor's coming to the opening," he said. "Show her a good time." Then he stepped onto the train, pulling the rolling bag behind him. The doors slid shut and the train pulled away. Zane was gone. All that was left of him was a Zane-scented "Ren and Stimpy" t-shirt and a Yomiuri Giants baseball cap at the bottom of a black garbage bag.

I headed back to The Last Stand to drop off Zane's remains with Vincent. A toasted, and slightly jovial Uncle Sal had his arm around the Nasty Drunk. They exchanged stale "farmer's daughter" jokes that could only possibly be funny to someone who'd been drinking sterno.

"Everything okay?" I asked Vincent.

"Yeah, fine," Vincent answered through clenched teeth.

"You'll be able to take care of this package?" I asked, handing him the black garbage bag.

"No problem."

"Hey, Vinny the Pooh," the Nasty Drunk called out, "how 'bout another round?" Uncle Sal broke up laughing.

"Good one!" Uncle Sal said. "I'm gonna use that one at our next family reunion. Much better than Vince the Wince."

Vincent winced.

"Why you call him that?" the Drunk slurred.

"Cuz he's such a wincing little pussy!" Uncle Sal screamed with delight.

The Drunk cackled and broke into song: "Vinny the Pooh, Vinny the Pooh. Wincing little pussy, hey, pour me another drink." Uncle Sal fell off his barstool.

"Holy shit," he said through the laughter. "I think I just wet my pants."

After witnessing this, I was so embarrassed for Vincent that I opted to drink at home instead. It wasn't even two o'clock yet. I was way ahead of schedule. I popped open a beer, sat on the couch and faced Julia's urn. We had one of our typical conversations. Whenever Julia got a little judgmental, I turned the tables on her. It was, after all, because of her that I had to develop the hare-brained scheme in the first place. Had she not left me, there never would have been the need.

Three o'clock rolled around. It was time to pick up Mittens/Aldonza from the cat groomer. When I arrived, the cat was already in her crate and the crate was covered with layers of black tulle. The groomer approached me dramatically and gestured wildly with her arms whenever she spoke. I couldn't decide whether to classify her as eccentrically odd or just plain scary.

"What came in as a meager alley cat is departing as a

majestic work of art," the groomer said as she shoved the shrouded crate at me.

"Is she alright in there?" I asked, beginning to unwind the tulle.

"Do not disturb her now. She needs her beauty rest. You may reveal her splendor in exactly one hour." Translation: the psycho overmedicated the cat and the sedative hadn't worn off yet. I took the transformed and entombed Mittens to The Last Stand.

The bar was locked when I got there. Presumably, Vincent had finally gotten rid of Uncle Sal and the Nasty Drunk, and was now taking care of the black garbage bag. I opened the door with the spare key that Vincent had given me and brought the precious feline cargo into the back room. I carefully removed the layers of the shroud. I opened the door to the crate and waited for Aldonza to emerge. Nothing. I looked inside. The cat was curled up into a tight ball. I tapped the crate a little. Still nothing. I flipped the crate on its side and pulled the cat out. Lying on the floor in front of me was a very groggy tiger cat with purple and yellow stripes and bright neon green whiskers. Her claws were each painted a different color. And she wasn't at all happy. She tried to stand up and walk but her hind legs weren't working. She staggered around, falling all over the place, as if she had Mad Cow disease. I removed my coat and crumpled it up into a makeshift cat bed. I picked her up and placed her on it. I gently petted her peroxided head and told her that she was a good girl. I looked up at the clock. It was ten past four. Zane was on his way to Tulsa. Good thing too. If he had witnessed this he definitely would have killed me.

CHAPTER SIX

A DEBONAIR HIPSTER stared back at me from the mirror. I checked him out from every angle. I practiced posing. I practiced looking detached and uninterested. In essence, I practiced being an ultra-trendy. It was now five-thirty. I had another fifteen minutes or so left to rehearse, then it was show time.

I called Tucker in to watch over Aldonza until she came out of her haze. For the first time in my life, I was glad to see him. He called me at a little after five to let me know that she was walking around without difficulty, and had found and used her litter pan. He also told me that Vincent still hadn't gotten back. I thanked him and told him to wait there until either Vincent or I returned.

At two minutes to six, I stepped into the trendy Last Stand Galleries. It was trendy because I was trendy and other trendy people would be going there; thus the dive bar that was once The Last Stand became trendy by default. I went directly to the back room to check on Mittens.

"Who's that handsome young man?" Tucker greeted me.

"How is she?" I asked.

"She's no longer cat-atonic . . . if that's what you mean."

I ignored Tucker and examined Mittens.

"That would have been cat-astrophic, don't you think?"

She seemed to be breathing normally, and she was walking without difficulty. I let out a sigh of relief and refilled her bowl with fresh water.

"I'm just joking with you, Harry," Tucker continued. "Can't you tell when I'm just 'kitten' around?"

"Any word from Vincent, Tucker?"

"Vincent Tucker? Who's that?"

"Tucker, I'm not a violent man, but I will reach down your throat and rip out your lungs if you don't answer my question."

"No, Harry. No word from Vincent."

"Thank you."

"Maybe the cat's got his tongue."

I was growing weary. And not just weary of Tucker, I was physically wobbly. Then I realized that, in all the excitement, I had forgotten to eat all day. My only nourishment had been coffee, whiskey and beer (in that order). I heard Julia's voice in my head: "Very nice, Harrison. Very nice."

The caterers arrived at ten after six. As they began setting up, I began sampling the cuisine. I was too hungry to wait. As I stuffed a fistful of finger sandwiches into my mouth, Teresa walked through the door. Dressed in a strapless black gown, with her hair pulled back into a tight bun, she was an exquisite vision—what Grace Kelly would have looked like if she were a disaffected, jaded brunette.

"Save some food for the guests, Harrison."

I tried to swallow quickly so I could respond, but the bread wasn't cooperating. Instead, I began to choke on it and coughed up some of the sandwich.

"Is the cat all set up?" she continued, in a rather annoyed tone. Tucker popped his head out from the back room.

"Cat-egorically speaking, she's doing just purr-fectly now," Tucker chimed in.

"What the hell is he doing here?" Teresa snapped.

I finally cleared my esophagus.

"He's helping me out until Vincent gets back. Your groomer really did a number on the cat. She's just coming to."

"How does she look?"

"Like a fright wig that was hit by a paint truck."

"Excellent," Teresa said.

"I'll betcha that Zane goes ballistic when he sees her," Tucker said. "You may have done some purr-manent damage." Teresa shot him a deadly look. But Tucker didn't interpret it correctly and continued speaking. "I think he's gonna take it purr-sonally."

"New rule, Tucker," Teresa said in a clipped and harsh tone. "You don't get to speak anymore. You've used up your word quota for the day." Tucker was silent. Teresa turned her focus on the caterers setting up. "What the hell is this? This is all wrong." She began ordering the caterers around, moving the tables and food. "Harrison, can't I trust you to do anything besides stuff your face?"

"But Teresa . . ."

"Is that alcohol on your breath?" she said accusingly.

"I haven't . . ."

"Just get in the back room and watch the cat . . . if you think you can handle that. And don't come out until you're sober." She motioned to Tucker. "This idiot and I will take care of everything else until my other worthless partner decides to show up." Tucker started to speak, but Teresa shot him another deadly stare. He interpreted this one correctly and clamped up immediately. I stood there dumbfounded. "What the hell are you waiting for," Teresa seethed, "an engraved invitation? Get back there. You're in the way."

I staggered into the back room, where I was confronted by the pained meowing of the scared and confused monster of a cat I helped to create; the one I promised to be responsible for. All for Teresa. All for Julia. All for nothing. What else could go wrong tonight? I was going to find out.

CHAPTER SEVEN

SHORTLY AFTER my back room exile began, I was joined by Vincent. He looked a little haggard and out of sorts. I couldn't ask him where he was or what he had done with Zane's clothing because Tucker kept coming in and out of the room, Teresa's newest minion. Vincent and I just looked at each other awkwardly, like two kids that were sent to detention; one for tardiness and one for drunkenness. Finally, Vincent broke the silence.

"That's one fucked-up-looking cat."

"She sure is," I answered. "I notice you're a little late. Nothing wrong, I hope."

"No, nothing wrong," Vincent said. "Things just didn't go as originally planned."

"Should I be worried?"

"I think you'll be pleasantly surprised."

My heart sank into my stomach. Vincent had improvised on the plan, which meant that it was time to worry. All he was supposed to do was dump the clothes from the black garbage bag into a garbage can on East 7th Street and Avenue B, right across the street from Tompkins Square Park. Since homeless people rummage through that particular garbage can all the time, the clothing was sure to resurface sooner or later. The police would run around trying to connect the dots and whatever they came up with would be fine with us. That was the beauty of the plan. The total randomness of it. We give the cops a crumb and let them make a cake out it. But now that plan was in jeopardy. Rather than follow the simple plan, Vincent had done something complicated—why else would it have taken so long?—meaning there was a very good chance that he left clues around that would ultimately point to us. But there was nothing I could do now. Nothing I could say. Just wait and see. And Tucker's continued presence wouldn't permit me to press Vincent any further. Pleasantly surprised? My liver did a somersault.

At ten minutes to eight, feeling reasonably sober, I gathered up enough nerve to pop my head out of the back room. The fashionably late conformist throng was still filing in. Teresa greeted each and every one of them with a hug and kiss, and each attendee reciprocated with a hug and kiss of their own. The amazing part was that Teresa loathed each and every one of them; but her loathing was only a fraction of how much she was despised in return. Hovering in the background, and looking incredibly out of place, was the police detective: Teresa's shadow. Günther and Giselle were surveying the art work, their faces sour in delight, certain that Teresa Traut's newest venture was doomed to failure and that they were completely justified in firing her. Other ultra-trendies perused Zane's work with equal acerbic enthusiasm. It was a good thing that Zane wasn't here to see it. I made a mental note to embellish these initial reactions when I recounted the story to him. Revisionist history can spare feelings.

There was one person who looked at the work thoughtfully and with a sense of wonder. She was unlike the others; she wasn't even remotely ultra-trendy. She wasn't ultra-anything. This unpretentious blonde-haired woman, who appeared to be in her late twenties, wore a simple yellow frock and very little makeup, which made her seem invisible to rest of the crowd, but not to me. She pored over each painting, unconsciously nodding her head, as if she were communicating with the pieces and vice versa. I just stood in the doorway watching her look at the paintings.

Her gazing at the paintings and my gazing at her were abruptly interrupted by the feedback from a microphone being too close to an amplifier. Teresa was ready to give her talk.

"Good evening and thank you all for attending," she began. "It's wonderful to see you all here. Welcome to the Last Stand Galleries and *Catharsis*, the art experience of Zane Burroughs and Ms. Aldonza." Polite applause ensued, coupled with enthusiastic clapping from the yellow-frocked blonde.

"I'd like to point out the players responsible for tonight's event," Teresa continued. "The owner and proprietor of the LSG, Mr. Vincent Pirelli." Vincent, who had emerged from the back room moments earlier, waved to the crowd.

"And our Director of Development, Harrison Spangler." I waved to the crowd. I received light applause and a couple of snickers.

"And, of course, the one human most responsible, Zane Burroughs." More polite applause. Teresa scanned the crowd, waited about five seconds.

"Can we get Zane up here?"

The crowd began to murmur.

"Harrison, where's Zane?" Teresa asked, while covering the microphone, knowing full well that her detective friend was watching.

"He hasn't arrived yet," I said.

"Fucking typical," she said exasperated. She was putting on a show and doing it very well.

"Zane's running a little late," Teresa addressed the crowd.

"If I'd painted this tripe, I wouldn't show up either," I overheard a semi-muffled voice from the mob.

Teresa grabbed my arm with one hand, and partially covered the microphone with the other. "Call that fucking flake, and get his ass over here now!" It was perfect. The sound carried into the microphone so that everyone in the audience could hear it.

I went into the back room and dialed Zane's number. I left my rehearsed message on his answering machine: "Hi Zane, it's Harry. We're all waiting here, and the festivities have already begun. Maybe you're already on your way, in which case I'll see you shortly, and you can disregard this message. But if not, get the hell over here ASAP. Teresa's really pissed off; and trust me, you don't want to get that bitch mad." The bitch reference was key. It added a touch of realism to the whole thing. But my brief euphoria of a job well done quickly dissipated and transformed itself into outright terror when I noticed that

I'd left the door to the back room ajar. And I didn't see Mittens anywhere.

I frantically dismantled the back room. I ran out into the gallery with my eyes to the floor. I was startled by Teresa: "Well, did you call him?"

"Huh?" I said, caught off-guard for the moment. "Oh, yes, I left a message. He's probably on his way as we speak." Then my gaze quickly returned to the floor.

"Harrison," Teresa interrupted my search again. "I'd like you to meet a friend of mine." I looked up at the police detective.

"Hi, I'm Ed," he said extending his hand.

"Harry," I said, extending mine.

"Why don't you keep Ed company, while I tend to the critics," Teresa said and quickly disappeared, while Detective Ed and I shook hands. We watched her go and then shared an uncomfortable silence. My eyes continued to scan the gallery in search of Mittens.

"Have we met before?" he asked.

"It's quite possible. I've met so many people at so many shows."

Another silence.

"Can I help you look for whatever it is you're looking for?" the perceptive cop asked.

A loud sneeze echoed from across the room.

"I think I might have just found it, Ed."

We pushed our way through the crowd to Teresa. She sneezed again. When Ed and I caught up to her she was in a conversation with Günther and Giselle, showing off one of the paintings, and sneezing each time she got too close to it. Teresa stared at us with a look that was a combination of incredulity and bottled-up rage.

"Could you boys give me a moment? I'm with a prospective buyer." Then she returned to Günther and Giselle with an occasional sneeze thrown in. Ed's face reflected the way I was feeling. He was under her spell, too.

"So, when do we meet this Aldonza?" Günther asked, stroking his goatee and staring off into space. He seemed thoroughly bored, but perhaps it was just his affectation.

"Harrison," Teresa said. "Could you bring Aldonza out? These people would like to meet her."

Ed must have picked up on the sheer terror in my eyes, because he followed me into the back room with great concern.

"Are you okay?" he asked. "Do you need an ambulance?"

"I gotta level with you, Ed. I can't find the cat. I accidentally left the door to this room open. Probably ran through the gallery and out into the street. Teresa's gonna rip my balls off."

"Look, there's no reason to panic. Someone would have seen the cat if it went into the gallery, right? There are just too many people out there not to notice."

"Have you taken a good look at that crowd? They're so jaded and self-absorbed, you could walk a pack of elephants through and they wouldn't notice."

"You've got a point there," he said. I began to hyperventilate.

"But," he continued, "if a cat is frightened, it's not going to go into a crowded room. I'd bet that it's hiding in here somewhere."

He was right. I hadn't even thought of that. I began to calm down.

"Let's seal off this room," he continued.

"You talk like a cop," I said.

"Is that meant to be an insult or a compliment?"

"Just an observation."

Detective Ed sniffed out the place. Within five minutes he located Aldonza. Hiding in the back of a closet, her eyes glistened when the light hit them.

Ed moved in to pull her out, but in the process, ended up discovering Vincent's stash of marijuana. Mittens must have been drawn to the scent and associated it with Zane. And now a cop had pulled out a felony possession-sized amount. I needed to say something. Something that would keep me from incriminating myself, while not tipping my hand that I knew he was a cop.

"Boy, that's a lot of pot," was all I could produce.

"Sure is," he answered. "Let's get the cat."

He moved in and grabbed her, let out a tiny scream, and then came out holding his own newly bloodied arm. Aldonza had multicolored claws and she wasn't afraid to use them. She hissed and retreated further into the closet.

"Maybe we should just wait for Zane to show up," he said.

A bead of sweat ran down the side of my forehead. I hoped that Ed wouldn't notice, but that wasn't to be. He was too perceptive for that. I covered quickly.

"Can't wait for Zane. Teresa needs the cat now to reduce the embarrassment of Zane being so late."

The cop pondered the situation. "What about his neighbor?"

"Whose neighbor?" I asked.

"Zane's neighbor. She introduced herself to Teresa when she arrived. Maybe she can lure the cat out."

"I'll try anything at this point."

"Wait here, I'll go get her."

Ed left me alone with the terrified, but ably equipped Mittens. He returned with Zane's neighbor in tow: the blonde-haired woman in the yellow frock. She had an innocence to her, coupled with a down-to-earth quality that was so sorely missing from everyone else in the gallery. I wiped the sweat from my hands onto the back of my pants, and extended a hand to introduce myself.

"Harrison Spangler. Pleased to meet you."

"Molly," she replied, taking my hand. Her hand felt like a slimy dead fish. Apparently I wasn't the only nervous one in the room. Ed took charge.

"It seems Zane's cat is a little frightened, and has hidden herself in the closet. We were thinking that maybe, since the cat knows you, you could try to lure her out."

"Oh, that shouldn't be a problem," Molly said. "She's such a gentle thing."

Ed showed her his bloody hand; the gentle thing's calling card.

"Oh my," she gasped. "Mittens did that?"

"Who's Mittens?" asked Ed.

"Aldonza," I answered. "Teresa thought it best to change the cat's name for the show. 'Mittens' didn't have enough oomph."

"Well, she's taken on a new personality with the name change," Ed said, looking at his hand.

Molly smiled nervously and shrugged, then made her

way toward the closet. "I'm sure she's just a little scared. Mittens . . . where's my kitty?" she said as she poked her head inside the closet.

"Holy shit! What the hell did you do to that poor cat?" she roared, practically frothing at the mouth. "Zane's gonna fucking rip your head off when he finds out what you did to her, you sick fucking asshole bastard!"

I had to say something. I wanted to just blame it on Teresa, but I couldn't; not with the sycophantic Detective Ed there. I had to take the blame for it myself. Stand up and tell her that this is the art world, baby, and that's what we do here. This was just a simple alley cat, who was now transformed into the toast of SoHo art circles. And that didn't come without a price. And if that price was Zane being upset because the cat's fur and nail colors were temporarily altered, so be it. Zane wants a show, he needs to make a sacrifice.

That's what I needed to say. Unfortunately, those words never passed my lips. The problem was this: I wanted Molly to like me. So I needed to find another villain. There was only one logical choice.

"It was all Zane's idea."

WE FINALLY REMOVED THE CAT from the closet by throwing a blanket on her and forcing her into the crate. Molly's idea. While we were throwing the blanket over the cat, Molly kept saying how she was going to give Zane a piece of her mind for allowing the transformation of Mittens. "Maybe that's why he hasn't shown up yet; he's afraid of what you'll do," Ed joked.

In the gallery, the show was a total flop. Aldonza garnered little attention, and she hissed at people from inside her crate. Between sneezes, Teresa made light of the situation to the guests by calling Aldonza a "moody feline artiste."

The show was now a little over three hours old, and the crowd was beginning to disperse. Teresa blocked the door, begging people to stay, saying that Zane should be here any moment.

"I hope he's okay," Teresa mentioned to Günther and Giselle. "I mean, he seemed so excited about the show, and then for him not to be here yet . . ."

"I wouldn't worry," Günther said smugly. "It seems Zane already knew what we all discovered tonight . . . that he's not much of an artist."

Before Günther and Giselle could leave, however, four uniformed cops came bursting into the bar/gallery.

"Who's in charge here?" one of the cops asked.

"What's the fucking idea?" Vincent said.

"Read it and weep," the cop said shoving a search warrant at Vincent. The cop walked over to Ed, as the other three made a beeline for the back room, with a very irate Vincent close on their heels.

"Thanks for the tip, Detective."

"What the hell?" Ed said.

"What's the matter? Is this the wrong place?"

"Wrong time. How'd you get a warrant so fast for a little marijuana stash?"

"Judge was working late tonight. Unofficially, it's war on drugs week, and he's handing out warrants to anyone who asks."

"Jesus," Ed said.

He looked meekly at Teresa. She was a volcano ready to erupt. And Ed knew he was going to be covered with some molten rock.

"I think, perhaps, we'll stick around a little longer," Giselle said, a wide grin plastered across her face. She and Günther sat majestically on a pair of barstools and enjoyed the ensuing police drama from their front row seats.

The three cops emerged from the back room, each carrying large amounts of marijuana. Vincent was handcuffed and ranting.

"It's not mine! It's not mine!" he shouted.

"Save it for your lawyer," one of the cops answered. "He might actually care."

"I'm telling you," Vincent pleaded. "It's not mine. I'm a legitimate businessman." Vincent looked at me as they were pulling him away. I could see in his eyes what he was thinking. He was looking for a fall guy, and there was only one obvious choice.

"It's Zane's stuff," he shouted.

And then something truly astounding happened.

CHAPTER EIGHT

MITTENS CAME OUT from hiding under my couch a little before seven a.m. I had just finished recounting the wild events of the evening to Julia over a nice big glass of bourbon. It was absolutely unfathomable to me that by the end of night Günther and Giselle had purchased Zane's entire collection for a hundred eighty-five thousand dollars. Julia seemed rather amused by it all. Especially how Teresa took credit for everything. "It was rather brilliant of me to invite Ed, wasn't it?" Teresa kept saying, completely unable to differentiate between clever meticulous planning and plain old dumb luck.

If she wanted to nitpick, it was actually Vincent who carried the day, with his uncanny magical ability to spin vengeful idiocy into gold. As the police were taking Vincent away, and he was laying the blame on Zane, the old Nasty Drunk came staggering into the bar looking for Pete to buy him a drink. He was dressed in a blood-stained Ren and Stimpy t-shirt and a Yomiuri Giants baseball cap. When Molly screamed out that Zane was wearing those same clothes that very afternoon, Ed decided to haul the whole lot of us in for questioning. The SoHo art world gossip machine kicked into gear at high throttle, replete with conjecture, supposition, and innuendo; and in no time, a mythic tale grew from Zane being involved in a drug deal gone bad to Zane being the target of a hit by a rival drug gang in a turf war. His art was no longer the synthesis of man and beast, but the reflection of his tortured soul from his secret life of crime and gang activity; this newly redefined commodity being 'gangsta' art. "Of course, placed in *that* context," Giselle explained, "these pieces are rather brilliant."

Teresa's cell phone rang several times while we were being questioned at the police station. Detective Ed was too afraid to ask her to turn off her cell phone, so she fielded calls at the precinct from various art dealers. The highest bid came from Günther and Giselle, and Zane's collection was transferred from The Last Stand to Reinhardt Galleries before we even left the police station.

The police were holding Vincent overnight. He'd likely be arraigned in the morning and then released on his own recognizance. The Nasty Drunk would remain until he was sober enough to give a statement. Vincent's improvisation proved fruitful. The Nasty Drunk had needled Vincent one time too many, and after Uncle Sal finally left the bar, Vincent pretended to be "Pete" and offered the Drunk a whole bunch of buy-backs. When the Drunk passed out, Vincent rolled him, stripped him of his clothes and replaced them with Zane's. The blood stains came from the Drunk. He had cut himself on a broken shot glass, so Vincent let him bleed on the clothing for effect. He dumped the Drunk in a nearby back alley and took the Drunk's discarded clothes to Tompkins Square Park. When the Drunk finally came to, he staggered back into the bar looking for some more free booze courtesy of Pete. Vincent's ultimate plan was to frame the Drunk for Zane's disappearance. It made absolutely no sense, but then again, it didn't have to. The Drunk wasn't going to remember anything. He was the perfect unreliable witness.

The police searched Zane's apartment, found his clothes laid out and ready to go, listened to the message on his answering machine from me inquiring as to his whereabouts (and warning him of Teresa's inclination towards evil bitchitude), and came to the unofficial conclusion that Zane had fallen victim to foul play. Mittens needed a new home, so I took her in. At least I was able to keep one of my promises to Zane.

Mittens rubbed against my leg and I petted her distorted fur. "You must be hungry," I said to her. I went to the kitchen and got a can of tuna. As soon as I pulled the pop top, Mittens went crazy; the sound and smell of the can opening set her off in a Pavlovian feeding frenzy. She began darting all over the apartment, leaping from the couch to the table to the floor to the couch. As I spooned her food into a bowl, my door bell rang. This caused Mittens to change directions and leap onto the bookshelves, toppling a few books in her wake.

"Harrison?" a voice called from the other side of the door. "It's Molly. Are you okay in there?"

I opened the door and greeted Molly with a bowl of tuna in my hand.

"Mittens was just getting frisky before breakfast. What brings you here?"

"I've been up all night. I need someone to talk to. I

figured you'd still be awake."

I offered her a drink, but she refused. I led her to the couch and sat down next to her. She seemed uncomfortable, but I wasn't sure whether it was because she was in my unkempt apartment, or because of what brought her to my unkempt apartment. After an interminable series of deep breaths and sighs, she spoke her mind.

"It's Zane," she said. "I just can't believe any of this."

"Any of what?"

"The drug-dealing, the cat abuse . . . just any of it."

She tapped her fingers against the side of her head while she twirled her blonde split ends.

"He was just so genuine, and all he cared about was his cat and his art. So how? Just how did this all happen?" she trailed off and buried her face in her hands.

I started sweating. I couldn't think of a thing to say to counter her. Anyone who'd ever met Zane knew he couldn't be the person Vincent and I had framed him to be. Hell, even Tucker expressed disbelief when Detective Ed questioned him, but Ed just figured Tucker didn't have a clue when it came to assessing human behavior; after all, how well could Tucker understand the human condition if he thought his jokes could make people laugh? But Molly wasn't Tucker.

"I don't know what to say," was my response. Probably the truest thing I could have said.

"But he DID do all these things," she said. "He had me so completely fooled."

"He had all of us fooled, Molly," I leapt in. Probably the falsest thing I could have said.

"I figured you would understand," she continued. "You were the only person all night that did anything noble."

I searched my soul to figure out what she meant, but came up empty. Luckily, she provided the answer.

"The way you went out of your way to take care of Zane's cat . . ." She couldn't finish her sentence, and covered her face again. Mittens had just finished devouring her breakfast and looked like she wanted more. I shamelessly decided to play up my newly anointed hero status.

"I'd better get her a treat. This can't be easy on her either." I nobly strode into the kitchen and heroically opened a package of cat treats. Mittens began her Pavlovian routine, leaping from the couch to the table to the floor to the bookshelves. But this time there were casualties other than books. Julia's urn crashed to the floor.

I was paralyzed. Frozen in my tracks. It took all of my strength just to look downward and aim my gaze in the direction of the crash site, where I viewed the remains of my life with Julia sprawled out across the living room floor. The cat had run away, tramping through bits of the ashes and leaving a trail of Julia's memory behind her. Molly came into view, stooped over holding the top of a discarded pizza box, a makeshift dustpan. She began to sweep up the mess, commingling it with bits of dried cheese and tomato sauce. Unable to find my voice, aside from a barely audible whimper, I remained stuck to the floor, as Molly swept Julia up, haphazardly tossing in bits of cat hair and extraneous household grime as well.

"Gosh," Molly said as she expunged Julia. "Why would you save all these cigarette butts? And they're all stained with lipstick." She paused. "Oh," she said, in an uncomfortable moment of realization. She stopped sweeping and placed the pizza box top on my kitchen counter and stepped away.

"Maybe I should go." She waited for a response from me, but I still couldn't speak. She walked to the door and opened it.

"No," I managed to spit out. "Please . . . don't." She closed the door and walked toward me. She grabbed hold of my arm, guided me to the couch and sat me down. We sat there without talking for about an hour. Molly sat next to me, holding my hand the whole time. She broke the silence.

"Do you have a picture of her that I can look at?"

I reached into my back pocket and pulled out my wallet. I dug deep behind my driver's license, years of receipts and my social security card before producing Julia's wrinkled photo. An action shot of her blowing a smoke ring, a lipstick-stained cigarette prominently displayed in her right hand.

"The cigarette butts are all you have to remember her by?" Molly asked softly.

Molly understood. She understood everything without my having to tell her. She'd just had a similar episode. She was madly in love with Zane, and now, not only was he gone, but the memories she had of him were all tainted by her newfound knowledge of him. The only difference between us was that her memories needn't be tainted. Zane was not a cat-abusing drug dealer, and unlike Julia, he was the same person she had always known and grew to love. My conscience was starting to get the better of me. I was going to have to tell Molly the truth sooner or later. Even at the risk of having us all end up in prison.

CHAPTER NINE

UNCLE SAL SENT HIS MOB LAWYER to plead Vincent out to misdemeanor possession, and a suspended sentence as a first-time offender. Vincent wore it like a badge of honor. It was a victory over Giuliani, the way he saw it. The Nasty Drunk couldn't remember a damn thing when he sobered up and the cops finally released him, retaining the hat and t-shirt as evidence.

There was nothing in the newspapers about Zane or Zane's show. Apparently not newsworthy. But in SoHo, there were no other topics worthy of discussion. Zane was HOT. And so was his art. Aldonza was the big loser, though. Teresa couldn't get anyone interested in the broken-hearted feline's solo efforts. The word on the street was that Günther and Giselle would be able to resell Zane's collection for almost twice what they paid for it. And that little news item—the fleecing of Teresa Traut— was ripping Teresa up inside. And the euphoria of pulling off our big scam quickly waned.

So now we were waiting for Zane to send us some new work from Mexico. But that wasn't something we were expecting for a while. Zane would have still been on the bus when Reinhardt purchased his collection. It would be quite some time before he would be settled down and producing in Mexico. With no prospects for any new pieces from Zane in the near term, and the marketing of Aldonza pretty much a failure, there was nothing left to do but split up our earnings. And after deducting for taxes and expenses, and then dividing by four, our shares were rather modest. Taking into account all the school days I missed to undertake the venture, my net profit came out to about five thousand dollars. Until we heard from Zane, there was nothing left to do but go back to substitute teaching.

I barely saw or spoke to Teresa over the next month. Just quick five-second phone conversations: "Heard from Zane yet?" "Not yet, Teresa." "Okay, keep me posted, Harry." Click. (She had stopped calling me "Harrison" a couple of days after the show.)

The Last Stand was no longer the bar it used to be. It became a shrine/tourist attraction for artsy types who had dreams of becoming the next Zane Burroughs, each pursuing Vincent to display his/her art work. I no longer felt comfortable drinking there. It was almost as if I had lost my home.

I stood in front of an un-air-conditioned classroom, withstanding an assault of paper clips being launched from rubber band-propelled rulers. With only a couple of weeks before summer break, and the unbearable June heat, the pelting was conducted with extra ferocity. I didn't really notice it, though. I was thinking about Teresa. Thinking about Molly. Thinking about Julia. I hadn't told Molly anything more about Julia and me. And although she seemed eager to find out, she understood that I wasn't ready to talk about it.

I was jolted back to reality when the bell rang, signifying the end of the class period, and the culmination of the paper clip pelting. The students gathered their weapons and made a hasty exit. The school principal poked her sweaty head inside the doorway.

"Mr. Spangler," she said curtly, as she surveyed the debris on the classroom floor, "some gentlemen here to see you." She stepped aside and Detective Ed and his uniformed lackey entered. She then left the room and closed the door behind her. I never got another call to substitute teach at that school again.

"Geez, Harry, hot enough for you?" Ed greeted me.

"What brings you here, Ed?"

"We've been going over all the statements we collected, and we're trying to fill in some blanks on this Burroughs disappearance. Thought maybe you could help."

"Sure," I said, pretending to be cheerful. "If you think there's any way I can help, I'd be glad to." I felt like a transparent villain on "Columbo."

Ed asked me a bunch of questions. My answers were about eighty-five percent truthful. I went over the last time I saw Zane at his apartment, when I picked up Mittens to take her to the groomer. I affirmed that Zane was wearing the "Ren and Stimpy" t-shirt and Yomiuri Giants baseball cap. I recounted my actions from the time I dropped the cat off to the time I picked her up. I left out the part about meeting Zane at the PATH station and handing off the black garbage bag to Vincent, of course.

After about fifteen minutes of questioning and story-telling, Ed and the cop closed their notebooks and thanked me for my time. I told them that if they had any further questions, not to hesitate to contact me.

"Actually," Ed said, "there is one more question I have." Uh-oh, I thought. Here comes a "Columbo" moment, when Peter Falk nails the bad guy in an inconsistency. I braced myself.

"When the cat was all screwed up from the sedative," he started, "you called Tucker in to look after her, right?"

"Yes," I said. "I was concerned about her, and didn't think she should be left alone."

"But, why Tucker?"

"I don't follow you."

"Tucker wasn't even scheduled to work that night. And he isn't the sharpest tool in the shed, if you'll excuse my saying so."

"I totally agree with you, Ed. Tucker was not the ideal cat-sitter. But I couldn't think of anyone else."

"What about Zane?" Ed asked, dropping the "Columbo" bomb. "It was his cat, after all. Who better to look after her?"

"Honestly, Ed," I said without missing a beat, "I was scared shitless about what Zane would do to me if he saw the cat like that. Calling Tucker was an act of self-preservation."

Ed laughed. "I knew there had to be a good reason for you to subject yourself to Tucker," he said. Then he shook my hand and left the classroom. I had survived the "Columbo" moment. Or had I? Ed returned ten seconds later.

"Didn't you say the grooming was all Zane's idea?"

"Pardon?"

"I thought you said the whole idea of transforming Mittens was Zane's idea."

"Yes. I did."

"Then why would you care what he would say or do? It was ultimately because of his decision that Mittens was in the state she was in, right?"

"I suppose so. I guess I never thought about it like that."

"Guess not," Ed said. "Well, see ya. Gotta meet Teresa for a lunch date. Don't want to keep her waiting."

Ed turned and left for good this time. One thing was certain: I'd found a worthy adversary, but unlike your typical "Columbo" villain, I wasn't going to underestimate him.

CHAPTER TEN

THE SCHOOL YEAR came to a merciful end. The summer months had been fairly uneventful. August rolled around, and we still hadn't heard from Zane. Teresa was getting mighty pissed. Especially since Günther and Giselle had managed to purchase all of Dean Grimaldi's work and were preparing for a dual showing along with Zane's pieces. Teresa, Vincent and I were all on the guest list for the opening of the Reinhardt Galleries' new show, *Victim/Victimizer: the tragic art of Dean Grimaldi and Zane Burroughs*. I invited Molly to join me for the opening, which she accepted without hesitation. She jumped at the chance to revisit with Zane's remains. Molly and I had a lot in common.

The Last Stand had undergone even more of a transformation in the last few months. Not only was it was no longer a fun loveable loser of a bar, the "LSG" was now tragically hip; a place for Artists on the Edge to grab a drink and theorize on the mystery of Zane Burroughs, and have furious debates about who, if anyone, would take his place in the gangsta art world. Vincent and Teresa played their parts in encouraging the artists. They'd even display some lucky artist's work every now and then. Just in case one of the artists actually had some sort of talent, Vincent and Teresa would be in a good position to grab up the commodity before Günther and Giselle.

Uncle Sal was also a new regular patron. Vincent told his uncle all about the scheme and it impressed the hell out of Sal. Gone were the days of "Vinny the Pooh" and "Vince the Wince." Uncle Sal was now looking for a position in Vincent's art scam syndicate, to get himself back on the crime wagon as it were. And since the current mob pickings were slim, he zeroed in on his nephew. He scrutinized all the artists in the bar, searching for the next Zane Burroughs.

As a result of the increased bar business, Tucker was getting a lot more work bartending. Uncle Sal and Tucker mixed like a snake and a retarded mongoose. Tucker was totally oblivious to the danger Uncle Sal posed. Instead, he'd discuss new routines with him, as he prepared his next "Solo Performance Experience." Uncle Sal twitched his mouth, which Tucker mistook as approval, instead of a nervous tick.

For me, the whole scenario was a nightmare. I didn't hang out there much any more, except to attend a conspirators meeting every so often. Those were the only times I'd get to see Teresa.

One night Vincent, Teresa and I sat around in the back room of The Last Stand trying to figure out what Zane was doing, and why he hadn't contacted us yet. There was no shortage of theories being tossed around. "He's stoned." "He hasn't finished a painting yet and is too embarrassed to call." "He's been on a three-month high and forgot." "He found out about the show and was pissed that we framed him as a drug dealer." "He got lost." "He's in jail." "He's been abducted by aliens." "He lost our contact information." "He's too stoned to dial a phone." "He's too busy watching a 'Lucy' marathon in Spanish." We ended up having some therapeutic laughs that evening, but it still didn't shake the clouds hanging over our heads—*what the hell was Zane doing?*

After the meeting I decided to have a quick drink at the bar. Tucker furnished me with a barmy beer and gave me a flyer for his newest one-man show.

"See you at the Solo Experience," he said. "It's definitely my most important work to date." I pocketed the flyer and a made a mental note to mix it in with Mittens's cat litter.

Uncle Sal nodded to me. I nodded back. It was some sort of conspiratorial signal that neither of us understood, but we did it anyway, just to remind ourselves that we were conspirators of some sort.

Artists talked bullshit all around me. Maybe that's where the term "bullshit artist" came from.

"Texturally speaking, he's no better than a poor man's imitation of a Pollack," one said of the lucky artist whose work was currently on display.

"I'm sure he's a big hit with the color blind," quipped another. Even though it was nighttime, and the bar was not at all well-lit, the majority of the patrons were wearing dark glasses and sporting trendy chin growths— even some of the women.

I chugged the beer and rushed back to my apartment, where I spent the night weeping. I was in mourning again.

I really had lost my home.

THE NIGHT OF THE REINHARDT OPENING, I picked Molly up at her apartment and we walked over to the Galleries. Molly said that she was nervous. She thought she was starting to get over Zane, and she was afraid that seeing his art again would send her back into a deep depression. I told her that it probably would and that she should get used to it. I knew from what I spoke. I had reconstructed my shrine to Julia on the bookshelf. Granted there were fewer cigarette butts in it, but the idea was the same. This was what I had to remember her by. Her mortal coil was elsewhere and I just had to deal with it. Nonetheless, Julia and I were now able to resume our nightly conversations.

Molly and I entered the Galleries and were greeted by the snooty Brat at reception.

"Are you on the list?" she asked in a culturally condescending way. She was terribly disappointed when she discovered I actually was on the list, and she was unable to turn me away. We entered the hallowed Reinhardt Galleries. We were now, officially, a part of the "in" crowd. We were now "behind closed doors." We looked at a few of Dean Grimaldi's paintings first. Nothing special in either of our humble opinions. We each silently concurred with Teresa's original assessment. Then we moved to the next set of panels where Zane's work was hung. The new location, theme and lighting gave them a fresh perspective. It was as if we were seeing some of them for the first time. And there was a very good reason for that. We *were* seeing them for the first time. There were about ten more paintings there than we had sold to them, each claiming to be a Zane Burroughs original.

Giselle and Günther appeared out of nowhere and greeted me.

"I see you're admiring our newest acquisitions," Günther beamed.

"Where . . . did you get these?" I managed to sputter out.

"Toronto."

"Toronto?"

"Yes," Giselle chimed in. "We have an exclusive contract with Drew."

"Drew who?" I asked.

"Why Andrew Burroughs, silly," Günther said.

"Who's Andrew Burroughs?" Molly asked.

"Zane's brother, of course," Günther snapped back gleefully.

"Naturally, we were surprised as anyone when he contacted us," Giselle commented.

"I had no idea that Zane even had an identical twin," Günther added.

I was speechless.

"He saved loads of Zane's paintings over the years," Giselle filled the brief gap of silence. "Apparently, he used to send many of his paintings home to their mother in Minnesota. How fortunate for us that he did."

Just then, Teresa entered the Galleries, accompanied by Detective Ed. Günther and Giselle saw their newest prey and pounced.

"Teresa, darling. Come look at our new exclusives."

Of all the theories we came up with about what had happened to Zane, we never stumbled upon this one. Zane was living out his sitcom fantasy. He out-Lucy'ed Lucy. He was now his own fictitious twin brother, collecting on his dead twin brother's art work. Truth is stranger than sitcoms.

Molly stared at the new pieces.

"It doesn't seem to have the same feeling as his other work," she said. "It's almost as if he was just going through the motions when he painted these."

I looked over at Teresa as Günther and Giselle gleefully recounted the story of Zane's identical twin brother. Teresa was all smiles. Never lost her composure. Never let her guard down. Not once.

Frightening, I thought.

CHAPTER ELEVEN

TERESA called an emergency conspirators meeting at The Last Stand. I took Molly home and Teresa got rid of Ed for the evening. Vincent sent Tucker home and closed the bar early. The Zane groupies were disappointed that they had to leave and constructed a makeshift shrine to Zane on the sidewalk in front of the bar. We sat around inside just staring dumbly at each other; waiting for someone to say something that would make it all better.

"Mother fucker!" Vincent finally offered.

"I never figured him for a double-cross," Teresa added.

I must admit, I was somewhat amused by it all. After we had framed Zane to be a cat-abusing, drug-dealing gang leader, such that he'd probably be arrested as soon as he showed his face in New York, we were actually indignant that he had chosen to sell his art from the safety of the Canadian side of the border. But what amused me the most was that by using the Lucy blueprint, the hare-brained scheme actually worked. What I did wonder about, though, was if he ever actually got on the bus to Mexico. Or had he planned this from the start? Maybe he took a bus to Buffalo and walked over the Rainbow

Bridge across Niagara Falls. I'd already framed a plan for him to get to Mexico; he could have applied the same thinking for a Canadian excursion. And that was eating at me. Was this his revenge for us not letting him take Mittens with him? And how did Molly really fit into this? He didn't ask her to come to the show until just before I met him at the PATH station. Was she a part of the plan? After all, it was Molly who screamed out that the Nasty Drunk was wearing Zane's clothes. It all may have been a tad too convenient. I started feeling less amused and more indignant.

"Let's get in touch with Drew Burroughs," I said.

"What are we going to say?" Teresa asked.

"Ask him how much Reinhardt is paying him and if it's really worth it to him."

"Why wouldn't it be?" Vincent asked.

"Because," I said, "we've got his cat. Maybe he'll cut a deal with us."

Teresa picked up the phone and called Toronto information. It was surprisingly easy to obtain the phone number of Andrew Burroughs. Teresa dialed the number. I told her to speak metaphorically to him; after my encounter with Ed, I didn't know if the phones were tapped or not; and I didn't want to take that chance.

"I got the answering machine," Teresa said.

She cleared her throat preparing to leave a message.

"Hello, Drew Burroughs? This is Teresa Traut. I just wanted to tell you that I saw your *twin brother's* paintings at Reinhardt Galleries tonight. I was just curious as to how much Reinhardt was paying for the art work; perhaps we can arrive at a deal for the next set of paintings you, ahem, uncover." Teresa could hardly contain her rage. "As you know, it's pretty cold up there in Canada. I'm sure you wouldn't want to be without your *Mittens* for much longer." She slammed down the phone, and began to pace. I looked at Vincent. We were each too scared to interrupt her to find out what she was thinking.

"Send him a paw," Teresa said.

"What?" I said.

"Send him one of the cat's paws. Show him we mean business."

"No," I said. "No fucking way. Let's at least wait to see if he calls back first. In the meantime, let's just split up his share of the initial take—that's forty-five grand—fifteen thousand for each of us."

Vincent chimed in: "I think we should send him the paw."

While it was true that I no longer felt the need to keep my promise to Zane to take care of Mittens, I had grown attached to the feline. She was good company. And she was a link to Molly. Molly. How did she fit into all this?

"Can we please just wait a bit before we do anything drastic?" I pleaded. "Give it a few days to see if he makes contact with us."

Vincent was all for carving up Mittens. Sort of like a "horse's head" Godfather fantasy for him. Yet another way to impress Uncle Sal. Thankfully, he and Teresa relented and agreed to my request. I had bought Mittens a brief stay of execution, but I had precious little time to come up with another plan. I had to see Molly again. I needed to find out what she knew and when she knew it.

"DID YOU FORGET something, Harrison?" Molly's voice crackled through the intercom at the entrance door to her apartment building.

"I need to talk to you about a few things. Can I come up for a little while?"

"My roommate's trying to sleep. She's got a job interview in the morning" the intercom squawked back. "Wait a second and I'll come down."

Molly joined me about ten minutes later.

"Do you mind walking?" I asked.

Molly said she didn't and we meandered through Little Italy and Chinatown. I picked up a hip flask of rum and a can of Coke, which we mixed together and shared during the stroll. We made small talk at first. I still couldn't find the right words. We walked further downtown and at Park Row decided to walk across the Brooklyn Bridge and look at the Manhattan skyline from across the East River. About halfway across the bridge, I gently broached the subject.

"Do you think we'll ever hear from Zane again?" I carefully observed Molly's reaction. She transmitted a quick, slightly coy smile, and then caught herself and put on a thoughtful expression.

"Oh Harrison," she said, "I don't think it's wise to hold out any hope. It's just more painful that way."

I tried to figure out the subtext to her statement. Was she saying that she was in on it all along and that Vincent, Teresa and I should just move on because Zane had beaten us; or was she talking about her own feelings for Zane? I had to know which. I grabbed her hand and stopped walking.

"Why did you smile?"

"What?"

"Before you answered me, you smiled and then covered it up. Why?"

"Because you're just so cute."

Huh?

"The way you ask me things in such a roundabout way. If you want to know if I'm over Zane, the answer is 'no.' It will probably always be 'no.' But I'm ready to move on."

Molly came in close, with her lips only inches from mine. The rum on her breath smelled wonderful. And in the middle of the Brooklyn Bridge, with the majestic Manhattan skyline as our backdrop, we kissed.

CHAPTER TWELVE

DETECTIVE ED called me the following week. I had once again been recounting my evening with Molly to Julia. I was gloating, actually. But Julia didn't seem at all jealous. Of course, why would she? After Molly and I kissed, we walked hand in hand for hours through lower Manhattan. She was just so genuine. She had totally allayed my suspicions about her. We said good night at her front door, so as not to disturb her slumbering roommate. We made plans to meet for a dinner date the following week, and tonight was the night.

Detective Ed said he was in the neighborhood, and wondered if he could drop by to chat. There were some pieces in the Zane puzzle that just didn't fit, and he thought maybe I could help. I told him he was welcome to come by any time. Three minutes later, Ed was in my living room.

I offered Ed a beer, just to see if he was off-duty or not. He accepted, and asked for a whiskey to go along with it, which piqued my interest. I opened a new bottle of Jim Beam for the occasion.

"So how's the investigation going?"

"Not really sure, Harry. I must admit, I thought you

might have been involved at first. I did a lot of checking up on you."

"Really? How so?"

"I've been talking to your neighbors."

"That's more than I've ever done."

"So I've learned."

"And what are their impressions of me? Let me guess, 'A quiet man, keeps pretty much to himself.'"

"No. They say you're a loud, drunk, annoying weirdo."

"That sounds accurate. So what's on your mind?"

Ed took a sip. Followed by a gulp. Rather dramatic.

"Everything I uncover seems to point to Teresa."

"Really?" I asked, without missing a beat. I was ready for Ed, and I knew anything he said to me, he would watch to see my reaction. "What makes you think that?"

"It all started coming together last week at the opening. First Dean Grimaldi, then Zane Burroughs. And they both end up at the Reinhardt Galleries."

Was he testing me? Or did he really believe it?

"It sounds a little far-fetched, Ed. Do you think they'd actually do something that obvious?"

"That's the beauty of it. They threw in just enough twists to keep us off the trail. Sure, they fired Teresa, but then she ended up selling them Zane's art work for a song. She splits that relatively small amount with you and Vincent, then behind your back makes a deal with Zane's brother to buy art for the Reinhardt. With the total resale of all that art work through Reinhardt, she's looking at splitting millions of dollars with Günther and Giselle; all through the guise of being their competitors."

"I don't know, Ed. I think you're just trying to get a rise out of me. Are you implying that Teresa is gypping me and Vincent out of millions?"

"No. I'm outright telling you that. I'm implying that she had something to do with Zane's disappearance and Zane's brother, Günther and Giselle were all in on it."

I stared at Ed. Did he actually believe what he was saying or was he trying to goad me into saying something incriminating? And was it possible that there was any truth at all to his hypothesis? Did Teresa actually leave that message for Zane? I only heard her side of the phone call. Did she really make the call, or was this part of a great big cover-up? She did allegedly obtain his phone number a little too easily for my comfort; especially considering he was fictional.

"Think about it," Ed continued. "Why was Teresa fired from Reinhardt?"

"Because she was indirectly responsible for Dean Grimaldi's suicide."

"And because she rejected his art work, which then went up in value."

"So?"

"She was fired from Reinhardt for rejecting his art work, yet they're displaying it exclusively. How'd they manage that if they rejected it?"

"They bought it up after his death. That's all well-documented."

Ed finished his whiskey. I refilled his glass.

"You can believe that if you want to, Harry."

"Why are you telling me all this?"

"Because we have something in common. We're both

in love with Teresa Traut and we're both allowing her to use us. I can't go through with this investigation any more than I could with Dean Grimaldi's."

"What do you mean? Dean Grimaldi was ruled a suicide."

Ed downed his second whiskey and staggered to my front door.

"Thanks for the hooch, Harry," he said, and then, in Columbo fashion added: "By the way, I'm heading up to Canada in a couple of days. Gonna have a nice talk with Andrew Burroughs."

He opened the door and gave me some more slightly drunken advice just before he left. "Stay the hell away from Teresa while I'm gone."

I FINISHED THE BOTTLE that Ed had started. A midday nap was exactly what I needed so I tried to drink myself to sleep. But my racing mind was having none of it. Mittens seemed to sense my unease and cuddled beside me. I was able to see what Zane found so sickeningly appealing about her. Was Teresa serious when she said we should send Zane a paw, or was that part of her ruse? And how far would she go with it? One thing was for certain: this cat was not going to be harmed again. Not on my watch. And when Ed told me to stay away from Teresa . . . why did he say that? Was he threatened by me? Did he believe that Teresa was developing feelings for me? Was it possible that Teresa was working with Giselle and Günther? And, most importantly, how much did he really know? Was he waiting to see how I responded to his threat about visiting Andrew Burroughs in Canada? A New York City police detective would be way out of his jurisdiction in Toronto. I figured it had to be a bluff . . . but then again, I couldn't be sure. Ed wasn't your typical New York City detective.

I alternated between worrying and drinking and that combination finally got me to sleep. I hadn't been sleeping fifteen minutes when a phone call from Vincent woke me.

"Harry. I think we gotta do the cat."

"We're not 'doing' the cat, Vincent."

"Me and Teresa were talking. She wants me to pick up the cat. She'd do it herself, but she's allergic and all. She thinks it's the only way Zane's gonna come across."

"There are other ways, without involving the cat."

"Like?"

"Are you sure you grew up in a mob family?"

"You want me to have his legs broken? Uncle Sal is available and willing."

"I'm not suggesting that, but I do think that would be more effective."

"I'll talk to Teresa about it. Uncle Sal could use some work."

"Still no word from Toronto?" I asked, even though I already knew the answer.

"Nope. Zane's not biting. And Teresa's lost her patience. She can't stand that Günther and Giselle's making more money than her."

"Is that a fact?"

"I said we should just forge Zane's paintings ourselves and sell those. After all, we got the cat. It'd be easy to just stick some fur into a blotch of paint."

"What did Teresa say about that?"

"She said forgery was a crime. That's one weird-ass chick, Harry. But very hot, you must admit."

Teresa's sphere of influence was growing. My conversation with Vincent ended without any real resolution. He was going to talk to Teresa again to see what she wanted him to do. Vincent was suddenly Teresa's messenger boy.

I substituted a shower for sleep, and got ready for my dinner date. All roads led to Molly right now. She was my salvation; she was my only way out. Now I just had to get her to agree to what I was about to propose.

CHAPTER THIRTEEN

WE ATE at a great little restaurant on Mulberry, right in the heart of Little Italy. There were loads of celebrity pictures covering the walls, but most of them were of the New York Yankees and Mayor Rudy Giuliani, Vincent's great nemesis. Vincent wouldn't be caught dead in the place, which is one of the reasons why I picked it. And they had good food, good service and a garden in the back, so we could dine al fresco.

"This is lovely, Harrison," Molly said as the maître d' seated us. I ordered drinks. Then we just sat there awkwardly, unable to come up with anything to say. We each mentioned how nice the weather was, and how nice it was to eat outdoors. We each mentioned how nice the waiter was, and how attentive the busboy was at refilling our water glasses. We had so much that we wanted to say to each other, but couldn't find the nerve to say. So when the dessert cart rolled by, we each jumped on the opportunity to comment on it.

"That tira misu looks amazing!" Molly said.

"Yes," I agreed. "And so does the profiterole. Shall we share an order of each?"

The awkwardness was painful. We had a major lack

of chemistry. We both were trying so hard to avoid the subject of last week's alcohol-inspired kiss on the bridge. Halfway through dessert, I finally asked if she'd mind stopping off at my apartment after dinner. I said I wanted to check on Mittens. She agreed, but she had to think about it. The fact that the date was not going well only strengthened my resolve.

"I like you, Molly," I said to her as we crossed the Bowery.

"I like you, too, Harrison," she replied politely.

We walked a couple of blocks without speaking further, and walked to my apartment building on Eldridge Street. We quietly stepped over a sleeping homeless man wrapped in a discarded Rugrats blanket and pushed through the eternally broken front security door to the building. Once we climbed the stairs and were safely inside the apartment, I sat Molly down on the couch. Such "romantic" surroundings were sure to get her in the right mood for what I was about to propose.

"This is really hard for me to say," I started.

"I had a feeling," Molly said, with a touch of despair.

"Just listen. I like you a lot, but there are things that we have to know about each other and about ourselves before we go any further."

"Such as?"

"Are we really ready to move on?"

"I am."

"Are you? What if Zane walked through that door right now and he had a really good excuse as to why he was gone?"

"We can worry about that when it actually happens."

"Suppose it did happen, though. What would you do?"

"Honestly, Harrison, I don't know."

"Well, I think I have a way for us to find out." I paced back and forth across the living room floor. I had her attention now, I just had to make the pitch.

"You know, I'm still not over Julia."

"Really?" Molly said sarcastically, glancing at the urn.

"That's why I'm sort of obsessed with Teresa. She reminds me of her."

"But Teresa is such a fucking bitch—pardon my French—but she is. Surely Julia was nothing like her."

"Perhaps," I said, "but emotions aren't rational things. They don't follow any sort of logic."

"I suppose not," she said.

"And there are things I still need to say to Julia, but can't; and never will be able to. But now I have the opportunity to say them to Teresa."

"So, you'd dump me for Teresa?"

"Not for Teresa; for Julia."

"I see."

"What if you were to see Zane's twin brother? If he was anything like Zane, do you think you could fall for him?"

"I don't know."

"Why don't you find out?"

There. I had said it.

"What?"

"Look, Molly. If you still have feelings for Zane, this is the way to find out. Go up to Toronto and see his twin brother. You probably won't even be able to tell the difference." Molly shot me a glance. I didn't know how to read it. I kept talking.

"If you feel nothing, then great, we have a future. But if you do feel something . . ."

Molly stood up and walked toward me. I braced myself for the impending slap in the face. But she gave me a peck on the cheek instead.

"You're ridiculous," she said. "Just drop the whole subject of Zane and Zane's brother right now."

I took a deep breath and slowly exhaled. I held Molly's hands and looked directly into her eyes. I wanted so much to kiss her then. But I used my mouth for talking instead.

"Suppose I told you that Zane doesn't have a twin brother. Suppose I told you that it was really Zane in Toronto; that he was framed by Vincent and Teresa and me; that it was all part of a big art scam gone wrong. And suppose I also told you that now Vincent and Teresa were looking to get even with Zane for selling his art to Günther and Giselle and were planning on sending him one of poor Mittens's paws to get his attention. And that the NYPD are planning on taking a little excursion up to Canada looking to talk with Andrew Burroughs. If I were to tell you that, would that change things?"

Molly turned pale. She just looked at me. Dumbfounded.

"And suppose," I continued, trying to keep my own emotions in check, "just suppose you were to take Mittens with you to Toronto, and you clued Zane in on what was going down. Zane would probably be eternally grateful to you, wouldn't he?"

After a moment Molly responded: "I suppose he would." She touched my left eye, and wiped a tear away from it—a tear I had no idea was even there.

CHAPTER FOURTEEN

I SAW MOLLY OFF at Penn Station two days later. It was the Thursday night before Labor Day, so the station was mobbed with people trying to escape the city for one last weekend before the unofficial end of summer. Despite the crowds, I insisted that Molly make the trip as soon as possible. I spent the previous day at the vet's office with Mittens, obtaining a health certificate so should could travel into Canada, and a tranquilizer in case Molly needed it for her on the train.

This was the only way it could be. I had to protect Mittens; and besides, it was best for the cat to be with Zane. And it was best for Molly to be with Zane. I didn't deserve either of them. And Molly certainly deserved better than me. Zane had bested me in all areas. But I felt no malice toward him. I even attached a note on Mittens's collar warning him about Detective Ed.

Molly and I said our goodbyes. I petted Mittens in her cat carrier and handed her over to Molly. I tried not to feel too sorry for myself; after all, I still had Julia and Teresa in my life, and that was plenty to keep me busy.

Molly got on the train. I went to a nearby sleazy Eighth Avenue bar to drink myself into oblivion. I drank a lot. Even for me. Countless shots later, I was not-so-gently being nudged to leave the premises.

"What a load of crap," I fired back. "After all the money I've invested in this establishment?"

The bartender pleaded with me to just leave quietly.

"Quietly? I'll leave quietly after you give me a buy-back. Vincent always used to give me a buy-back every third round."

A burly hand grabbed my collar, led me outside and unceremoniously deposited me at the curb. Across the street I saw another pub. I took it as a sign.

CHAPTER FIFTEEN

A WONDERFUL DRUNKENNESS came over me at the new pub. It was an almost perfect buzz. Almost, because it didn't accomplish its primary directive. When you have a photographic memory, how much must you imbibe, if you're drinking to forget? Quite a paradoxical quandary. They never asked that question on the I.Q. test. That's why the test is bunk. That was the only question with any significance in my life and I had no answer for it. I envy amnesiacs.

I staggered home many hours later, and, predictably, found Detective Ed waiting for me in front of my building.

"Eddie-baby," I said with drunken exuberance, "I thought you were off to Canada."

"Let's get you some coffee, shall we?" Ed said as he grabbed hold of my elbow.

"No. Not yet," I said. "I'm almost happy now. Don't take this away from me."

"Perish the thought," Ed said. "I wouldn't think of it."

He helped me upstairs. The last thing I remembered before passing out on the couch was Ed making a phone call.

THE SMELL of freshly brewed coffee aroused my senses. I lifted my head, and quickly regretted doing so. I remained lying on the couch, gathering my thoughts, and getting my bearings. I glanced at my watch and was barely able to read it. It was around midnight; or was it noon? Ed appeared, hovering over me with a cup of coffee in his hand.

"Feeling a little better?" he asked.

I pushed myself up into a sitting position and took the coffee from him. I looked up at him skeptically. I had been very drunk. I hoped I had been tight-lipped, as well as tight. I took a sip and felt the burn.

"What brings you here, Ed?"

"Just playing some hunches," he said, pulling out a cigarette and lighting it. Nervy.

"I'd appreciate it if you didn't smoke in my apartment."

Ed looked at me with feigned shock.

"Sorry, Harry," he said, with mock remorse. "I just figured you wouldn't mind." He strolled over to bookcase. "After all, you've got this fancy ash tray here." He tapped Julia's urn. Then he extinguished his cigarette and tossed it into the urn. He watched for my explosion, but it never came. I was too hungover and too scared.

"You don't mind me commingling my butt with Julia's, do you?"

He watched for my reaction. I gave none. I said nothing.

"Those *are* Julia's cigarettes, aren't they?" he prodded.

I continued to say nothing.

"Computers are wonderful things, Harry. Just enter a name down at the precinct and it's amazing the things you find." He paused. "You can jump into this conversation at any time, you know."

I said nothing again.

"It's almost ten years now since Julia got that restraining order against you. September 26th to be exact. Hey that's a few weeks from now . . . how are you planning on celebrating the anniversary?"

I didn't like Ed any more. Not in the least.

"You know what the first thing was that tipped me off to you being a stalker? The first time I met you at the Reinhardt Galleries. You were decked out in some Canal Street knockoff designer apparel, putting on some fake sort of almost British accent, asking around for Teresa Traut. Said you had some sort of appointment with her, didn't you?"

I stared at Ed. My liver did a backflip.

"Of course, I followed up on that. Had to. That's what any cop who's worth his salt would do. And of course it turned out to be a lie. A few days later I was questioning Teresa at her apartment. My partner left early that day. He did a little snooping around and gave me a call at Teresa's. Just wanted to let me know that the weird fake British guy from the Galleries was standing across the street, drinking out of a paper bag. 'Looks like this chick's got herself a stalker' I thought to myself."

Ed crossed into the kitchen, picked up the coffee pot and refilled my cup for me.

"How's the coffee, Harry?" he asked. "Not too strong for you, I hope. I wasn't sure how you liked it."

"Coffee's fine, Ed," I managed to blurt out.

"So then Teresa starts concentrating on Zane and his work. You don't really get to see her. Zane's taking up all her time. He's in your way."

"Stop right there," I said.

But he didn't. He kept on talking. "Zane's in your way so you get rid of him. Still not sure how you did it, but that's okay. I don't need to produce an actual body to get a conviction. Just opportunity and motive. So, you get rid of Zane on the day of his show, knowing you can get a little extra cash for his art work if it's well timed. But lo and behold, you still aren't getting to see Teresa. Damn shame she's allergic to cats. Otherwise there'd be a chance you could get her over to your apartment. Where is the little darling kitty, by the way?"

I couldn't say that Mittens was on a train to Toronto. Not now. I cursed my wretched sense of timing.

"She's not here anymore," I managed to say.

"I know. I saw you leaving with her this morning, but she didn't come back with you. Just out of curiosity, what did you do with her? I hope you at least found a nice home for her. I'd hate to think of you as a cat killer, too."

"Hey-"

"It's okay, Harry. I understand. Your obsession with Teresa is hard for you to control. It all fits a pattern. You may even be able to get off on some sort of an insanity plea."

"Both Zane and the cat are alive and well," I blurted out.

"Really? Well, how would you happen to know this? I mean, if you knew something about Zane's whereabouts and didn't tell me, you'd be obstructing a police investigation; you know this don't you?"

I was fucked. I had to produce Zane, regardless of the consequences. The scam would have to be exposed. The problem was that Molly was on her way to warn Zane, and they would probably disappear all on their own. But I had to produce Zane. The next twenty or so years of my life depended on it.

"I think you should talk to Drew Burroughs," I said. "I think he may be able to shed some light on everything."

"Can't seem to get in touch with him. We called all day yesterday and all day today. Finally phoned up the Toronto police department to check on him for us."

"Let me guess," I said. "They couldn't find him and had no record of him."

"Oh no, Harry. They found him. Most of him at least. He was executed gangland style. Haven't found his head or hands yet."

It had been months since I'd thrown up. My streak came to an abrupt end.

CHAPTER SIXTEEN

TUCKER poured me a double bourbon with a tequila chaser. I was still in shock. I didn't know whether Vincent sent Uncle Sal, or if he did in Zane himself. It didn't really matter though. I felt responsible. Plus Molly was en route to finding her one true love beheaded.

Ed was waiting for me to turn myself in. In other words, he didn't have enough evidence to book me and hold me. But who knows what else he would turn up? Certainly, the restraining order didn't help my cause. But Teresa was different than Julia. I gave up on stalking Teresa as soon as I came to realize that she wasn't at all like Julia. Not really, anyway. I suppose that initially the resemblance was so strong, I immediately fell into my old ways, which happened to include stalking, I must confess. That was ten years ago, and I still hadn't recovered.

Tucker said he was expecting Vincent shortly. I had Tucker place a call to Teresa requesting her presence, and that it was important. I wanted to know whether Teresa was calling the shots, or if Vincent had decided to improvise on his own again.

But mostly, I thought about Zane. An artist that I corrupted with the temptation of fame, stardom and money, which led to the path of greed, deceit and ultimately death. He was Dr. Faustus to my Mephistopheles, except that I never wanted his soul. I just wanted to get closer to Julia, in the earthly form of Teresa Traut. The similarity between Teresa and Julia was that they both held all the strings. Teresa controlled me, she controlled Vincent, and she surely controlled Ed. And her influence in the art world controlled Zane. How could we all be so easily manipulated?

"TGIF," Tucker offered as he poured me a beer.

"Doesn't matter to me," I said. "I'm not working."

"But you will soon, right?" Tucker said. "Labor Day weekend. This is the last hurrah."

Last hurrah, indeed. I glanced over at the goateed freak that was inhabiting my former barstool. I felt sick to my stomach and returned my gaze to the narrow focus of my beer glass.

Teresa and Vincent arrived five minutes apart. Tucker remained at the helm behind the bar, and we moved to the back room. I swiftly and succinctly opened the meeting with three simple words: "What the fuck?"

"Communication breakdown," Teresa said. "I was just going through a bunch of 'supposes' and 'what ifs', and Vincent took it to the next level."

"Hey, you asked me what a fair price for a hit was," Vincent countered. "I told you I was connected and could get it for you at a greatly discounted rate; and you said 'well what are we waiting for then'."

"I was making a joke. Goddamnit! Why the fuck would I want him dead? He can't produce art that we can sell if he's dead!"

"We could forge it."

"I don't like forgeries. It's an insult to art."

"But it isn't art, it's Zane's crap. We could forge it easily. And we still have the cat, so we can add the fur to it."

"Maybe," Teresa said.

"Excuse me," I interrupted, "but do either of you realize the seriousness of what has happened? Your buddy Ed has been badgering me nonstop since Zane's disappearance, and he's ready to arrest me on suspicion of murder. And now we don't have a live artist to produce in that happenstance. And if I come clean and tell him the truth, then we'd have an even bigger motive for murder, which we ended up committing!"

Vincent and Teresa looked at me uneasily.

"What do you mean, if you come clean?" Vincent said.

"You're not considering going to the police, are you?" Teresa added.

I immediately regretted what I said. I could see in each of their faces that they didn't regret Zane's death on any other level than the financial repercussions. And now they suspected that I may be the weak link in the conspiracy; and a conspiracy is only as strong as its weakest link.

"I'm not going to the police," I said, trying to cover my earlier indiscretion. "The police are coming to me. I would never give us up."

Teresa exchanged glances with Vincent and then gave me a long look. "Okay," she finally said. "Don't worry about Ed. I'll take care of him. I'll see to it he leaves you alone."

"Thanks, Teresa," I said.

"Now, this forging paintings idea," she continued. "Not gonna work. Look, since we now know that there will no longer be any more Zane Burroughs pieces being uncovered, it may be time to introduce some solo work from Aldonza expressing her grief. I think we can make that work. Maybe we can use some of these other asshole artists that have been hanging around here. Aldonza was Zane's muse and collaborator, now she can collaborate with another local artist."

"I like it," Vincent said. "And if perhaps this new artist meets with an unfortunate accident . . ."

"Very nice," Teresa added. "We could get a curse thing going; like the Blair Witch only with a cat."

"And a busy Uncle Sal is a happy Uncle Sal," Vincent laughed.

"Go get the cat, Harry," Teresa said. "Let's match her up with one these artists here."

"Dead artist roulette," Vincent added giddily.

I froze. Didn't know what to do. If they knew I sent the cat away, they'd know I couldn't be trusted. I knew what Uncle Sal did to Zane. I would be next.

"Just bring the cat," Vincent said. "We're not gonna hurt her. Honest. She's our new money-maker."

I said my goodbyes and calmly walked out of the bar without looking back. One hundred yards down Spring Street, I broke into a cold sweat. I was totally fucked.

CHAPTER SEVENTEEN

I WENT directly to Molly's apartment to see if her roommate had heard from her, but no one was home. It was essential for me to get in touch with Molly. I had to get the cat back. I headed home, fretting the entire way and arrived at my apartment drenched in a pool of my own perspiration; New York in late August is a brutal time of year. And this particular August was especially brutal on me. I was glad that I only had to endure a few more hours of the wretched month, even though September didn't provide a great outlook at the moment. As I keyed into my apartment, my next door neighbor popped his head out.

"Hey neighbor," he said gleefully. I don't believe I'd ever spoken one word to him in my life, nor he to me. He picked a hell of a time to make first contact. "I've been on tour all summer—we were doing an all-male version of *Gypsy* up in Vermont—and I just got back this morning."

"That's very nice," I said, unlocking my door.

"I played Baby June," he offered unsolicited.

"Welcome back," I said, pushing the door open.

"Yeah, great to be back. I've been away since Memorial Day. The post office was holding my mail for me," he continued. "There were a bunch of packages that were addressed to you with my apartment number on it. Wait a sec."

The drag queen disappeared into his apartment. He emerged with three packages. I thanked him and took them into my apartment. He was still talking when I shut the door behind me.

The packages were all from Zane. They had Juarez postmarks, and were sent in June and July. He had addressed them with the wrong apartment number, and the mailman wasn't savvy enough to put them into the mailbox with all the other mail addressed to Harry Spangler. My tax dollars at work.

I unwrapped them, and stared at a breathtaking collection of paintings by the late Zane Burroughs. There were notes enclosed with each shipment. "Having a great time. Let me know when I can come home. Give Mittens a big kiss from Daddy," the first one said. "Why haven't you responded? Is it safe yet?" the second one said. And "What the fuck, Harry? Have you forgotten me? Don't make me do anything rash," was enclosed in the last one. I surveyed the paintings. Brilliant colors and rich textures accentuated each of the pieces. Mexico agreed with him. It was easily Zane's best work ever. Not like those rush jobs he put together up in Canada. Zane had obviously gotten pissed off that we never responded, and thought we were double-crossing him. That's when he must have decided to go to Toronto, slap some paint on a few canvases and sell them off to Günther and Giselle. And in doing so, Teresa, Vincent and I interpreted that as him double-crossing us, which led ultimately to his decapitation. All because he wrote "3F" instead of "3E" on the mailing label. So in the long run, Zane's was just another in a long line of postal-related homicides.

Molly called me collect from Albany. She was switching trains and would be back in New York in about three hours. I begged her to come directly to my apartment with Mittens. Things were starting to go my way. Although I rued the fact that Zane was no longer with us, at least I had solid evidence that he had been alive and well in Mexico. Plus, I had a rather valuable art collection. And no one knew about it but me.

I SPENT the next three hours cleaning my apartment, getting ready for Mittens and Molly's arrival. It was going to be a new beginning for all of us, and stripping away the filth from our previous existences was cathartic and symbolic in addition to being just plain hygienic. When I finished, the apartment sparkled. Even Julia's urn looked cheerful.

I poured myself a victory beer and plopped down on the couch. I was celebrating a guilty pleasure. I was going to have Molly and Mittens for myself now, but at Zane's expense. Yet another instance in my life where full happiness was denied. The doorbell rang a few minutes later. I threw the door open in anticipation, but was startled to find Vincent and Teresa on the other side. And they did not look happy.

"I was just talking to Ed," Teresa began. "You know, to get him off your back, just like I said I would. Because we're partners and that's what partners do."

I didn't say anything.

"And he told me something that I found pretty extraordinary," she continued, smiling through gritted teeth. "He told me that you no longer had the cat. And the fact that I'm standing in your doorway and I'm not sneezing, leads me to believe that he was telling the truth."

"The cat will be here any minute," I said. "She's on her way as we speak."

Teresa inhaled deeply. "Smells like she's been gone a while. Not even a trace of her according to my allergies. And my allergies don't lie."

"That's because I just cleaned the apartment," I explained.

"Let's go inside and talk, Harry," Vincent said.

"Not now," I said, placing myself between him and the doorway. Vincent tossed me away as if I were a crumpled piece of paper. I hurtled backward and crashed into the coffee table. Teresa and Vincent entered and closed the door behind them. Teresa stopped in her tracks when she saw the canvases.

"You double-dealing son-of-a-bitch," she said. "You traded the cat for the paintings, and didn't tell us about it."

"No," I said, "that's not true."

"Shut up," Vincent said, and punctuated it with a slap across my face. I shut up.

Teresa looked at the paintings, more exuberant now than angry. "Come on," she said to Vincent. "Let's take these out of here."

"What do we do about him?" Vincent asked, gesturing

to me.

"I'm not sure yet. Maybe he's learned his lesson," she said, then looked me right in the eyes, "in which case, we won't need to do anything. But if he hasn't . . . maybe a certain uncle of yours can educate him."

She broke off her stare. Vincent sneered. They gathered the paintings and left. "For a genius, you're not very smart," Vincent said to me on the way out. "Don't get any more bright ideas, okay?"

I went into the bathroom and washed my face. My nose was bleeding, and I had red marks on my cheek and neck that were approximately the size of Vincent's fingers. I wondered how long Teresa and Vincent were going to let me live. I was the only person who could implicate them in Zane's murder. I was the only one who knew about the hare-brained scheme. I was the only one standing in the way of their big payday. I knew I could expect a visit from Uncle Sal.

Forty-five minutes later, Molly arrived with Mittens. There were no happy reunions. We both broke down and cried to each other. I told Molly everything about the scam. And while I was in confession mode, I even told her about Julia. How I stalked her. How she got a restraining order out against me and ultimately moved away. How I convinced myself that she died of lung cancer so I wouldn't feel the urge to travel the country trying to track her down. And Molly understood. Little had I known that Molly and I were such kindred spirits. She confessed that she'd done a little stalking of her own. In fact, she moved into her apartment specifically to be near Zane. The reason she was able to identify the Drunk in Zane's clothes so easily was because she was so obsessed with Zane. So there we stood—two complete social disasters, waiting for a mafia uncle to come-a-knockin'. We held each other. I felt closer to Molly at that moment than I'd ever felt to Julia. Perhaps, we were each beginning to find a new object of our obsession, or perhaps this feeling was genuine, and dare I say, normal. Maybe we could run away together. Just Molly and me; leave all of our ghosts behind us.

But my daydreaming was interrupted by a knock on the door. Molly squeezed my hand. We both calmly walked to the door and opened it. We expected to see the face of Death at the other side. And we weren't wrong. The late Zane Burroughs was staring right at us.

CHAPTER EIGHTEEN

THE ONE THING that made the Lucy episode most unbelievable was that Danny Thomas posed as his own brother, and collected his share without providing any proof of who he was. (In the episode, they accepted that he must be his brother based upon a similar proboscis.) The reason that Zane was able to pull this off was the fact that he really did have a twin brother—a twin named Andrew who really did have some old paintings of Zane's from years back. A twin brother who had just been brutally murdered in Toronto. And Zane knew nothing about it. He'd been in Mexico all this time, getting stoned and painting. His reference to doing "something rash" was simply coming back to New York before we told him to. After the teary reunion between Zane and Mittens, I filled him in on all that had transpired. He just took it all in, and spoke softly when he had finally processed all the information.

"So, my brother is dead?" he asked.

"I'm so sorry, Zane."

"Don't be," he countered. "When he heard that I was missing, the only thing that bastard did was try to make a quick buck by selling my old paintings. He didn't shed any tears for me. I'm not going to shed any for him."

There was a long silence after that. Zane's tongue began to involuntarily protrude from his mouth. Obviously something else was on his mind.

"And I'm a drug-dealing gang leader?" he finally asked.

"If it's any consolation," I offered, "you're also a well-regarded artist with a very successful show at the Reinhardt Galleries."

"Not really the way I wanted it to happen," he said.

But it happened nonetheless. In the long run, there was a modicum of success. Teresa launched a new star and recovered her reputation; Vincent got in touch with his criminal roots; and Zane was now a famous artist. And I got to meet Molly. But now Molly was in the presence of Zane, and I knew how this was going to play out; how it had to play out. Molly would follow Zane to the ends of the earth. Just as I would have with Julia. And Zane certainly wasn't the "restraining order" type.

So now it was time to come up with a plan. Ed was on my ass, Teresa and Vincent had Zane's new pieces, and Uncle Sal was likely to make a visit. Zane was my ace in the hole. Having him alive and well helped us immensely. The only person it damaged, paradoxically, was Zane. His art work's value would plummet because of it. It was time for a brand-new hare-brained scheme.

"The first thing we have to do," I said, "is disappear. No one can know that Zane is alive. And Mittens can't be here either. We all have to lay low. Maybe Teresa and Vincent will think they've scared me out of town."

"Won't Ed come after you?" Molly asked.

"Yes," I said. "I do believe that he will."

I grabbed a few essentials, and we put Mittens back in her carrier. I sent Molly out to hail a cab. I told her to walk a few blocks first, in case someone was watching the building, and have the cab pull up in front. As soon as it did Zane, Mittens and I darted into the taxi.

"Where to?" the cabby asked.

"I need you to take us to Jersey," I said. "Newark Airport."

"Ten bucks over the fare and double tolls," the cabby said robotically.

"Fine," I replied, and the cab took off.

"Where are we going, Harry?" Zane asked.

"I'll let you know when I figure it out," I said.

WE SAT at the airport bar, having a few cocktails. Zane and Molly seemed a tad impatient, but I told them that this was an integral part of the plan. And it was. I needed a drink if I was going to come up with a brilliant and well-thought-out scheme. I had no intentions of getting on a plane. I figured if Ed or his sidekick were watching the apartment, they'd jot down the cab's number and find out where he took us. The airport would be a perfect place to lead him. It would occupy a great deal of his time trying to figure out what flight we ended up on. After I finished my drink, I hopped off my stool and led Zane and Molly to the Avis car rental counter. I had Molly rent a minivan (suitable for sleeping, if necessary), while we waited for her in the parking lot. When everything was in order, we left the airport. Molly asked where the hell we were going.

"Jersey shore," I said. "Where better to blend in on Labor Day weekend?"

WE COULDN'T get a room anywhere, of course, so we hung out in the van. Molly's non-stop fawning over Zane was beginning to get to me. And since we had to keep a low profile, I needed to stay in the minivan with them. And it made it that much harder to come up with a plan of action. All I could reason thus far was that Vincent and Teresa would probably try to sell the new pieces soon. And probably at Reinhardt. But what to do with that scenario?

"I think I should just show up at the Galleries," Zane kept offering up as his solution.

"Yes, Zane," Molly said each time he mentioned it. "That's a wonderful idea. You are just so brilliant."

"And where would that get any of us?" I finally replied. "It would make us all complicit in a fraud scheme, and then Vincent and Teresa would really want to seek revenge."

"What if I pretended to be my twin brother?"

"Because he's dead and everyone knows that."

"I could pretend to be one of a set of triplets."

"You still can't let this Lucy episode go, can you?"

"It inspires me."

"Zane, it may be high time to find a different model to follow. Lucy isn't cutting it anymore."

"Why not?"

"Lucy never had any beheadings in her show. Just

didn't get past the censors, I suppose."

Zane began to giggle.

"Do you find familial decapitations amusing?"

"Naw, I was just remembering the end of the episode."

"I thought it ended with Danny Thomas pretending to be his brother and collecting the money."

"It did, but before that-" Zane broke into hysterics. Molly began to giggle too. It was an infectious laughter that I was totally immune to. I waited patiently while the laughter came to a crescendo, subsided and then gathered up new momentum. I wanted to hang myself. And Molly didn't even know what the hell was so funny. But if Zane thought it was funny, that was good enough for her.

"Done?" I asked when the third wave of laughter seemed to have died down.

"Yeah," Zane said, dabbing his teary eyes. "See, Danny Thomas needs to paint a lost masterpiece for this auction after they think he's dead. So he ends up painting a nude portrait of Lucy, and the guy who plays Mr. Mooney on the 'Lucy Show' outbids everyone and buys it sight unseen. So when the painting is revealed and he sees it's of Lucy, he goes ape shit."

"Mr. Mooney bought it?" Molly asked with awe.

"No, same actor, different character. This was on 'Here's Lucy'—he played Lucy's Uncle Harry on that show."

"Uncle Harry, huh?" I said, half to myself.

I thought for a moment.

"Do you think you could paint something for your Uncle Harry, Zane?"

"Like what?"

"A tribute to Lucy."

Then I began to laugh. I finally got the joke.

CHAPTER NINETEEN

MOLLY AND I strolled along the boardwalk while Zane painted in the van. It was crowded. It was the last weekend of the summer, before all the kids had to return to school. There would be little need for me to substitute until October, which was when the regular teachers usually began to call in sick. Somehow they're always healthy enough in September.

Molly and I played about twenty games of Skee-Ball in the boardwalk arcades. We scored enough prize tickets to qualify for a plastic kazoo that said "Greetings from Asbury Park, New Jersey." Molly hummed some tunes on the kazoo as we leaned against a rail on the boardwalk and watched the ocean.

"What song are you playing?" I asked her, attempting to make conversation.

"Under the Boardwalk," she said. "By the Drifters."

"I guess that's what we are. A couple of drifters."

"Except we're *on* the boardwalk; not under it."

"Yes," I agreed. "Good point."

Conversation attempt number one had failed.

"The ocean looks beautiful, doesn't it?" I tried again.

"Yes, it does," she answered.

Silence.

Attempt number two met with similar results to attempt number one. "Third time's a charm," I thought to myself.

"What the hell do you see in Zane, anyway," I blurted out. Molly took notice. Finally a conversation starter with results.

"How could you ask me that?" Molly countered.

"He ignores everything you say and do. You could be dancing naked in front of him, and he wouldn't turn his head away from the television, even during a commercial. Why don't you just call it quits and move on?"

"Not until he takes out a restraining order," she said, practically spitting.

I was having trouble letting Molly go. Obviously. And I was fool enough to think I could talk her out of her obsession. I may have just as well been trying to get Zane to condemn marijuana and sitcoms. But those precious few moments on the Brooklyn Bridge that Molly and I had shared were unlike anything I'd experienced before. It's not as if I'd been a great romancer thus far in my life. In fact, my sexual conquests totaled somewhere between one and three, depending on how one defined the term "sexual conquest." Julia was not among the three. But she was aware of them all. I told her everything in an attempt to make her jealous. Didn't work. She couldn't have cared less.

"Sorry," Molly said, breaking my train of thought.

"About what," I asked?

"The restraining order comment. That was out of line. I know you're just trying to look out for me. To protect me from being hurt."

Another reason I liked Molly. She saw the good in people, even if it didn't exist. Thinking I was just looking out for her, when I really just wanted her for myself was a perfect example.

"Let's just go back and check on Zane."

We swung by a newspaper stand and picked up a New York paper to check for art news. I knew that Teresa and Vincent would try to push the paintings they stole from me, and I wanted to find out when and where. It was difficult to get any news, though and there was nothing in the newspaper. I had Molly call Reinhardt Galleries to inquire about any new shows. They were even more aloof over the phone than in person. But we eventually got the information we needed. New Zane Burroughs pieces on display this Wednesday evening. By invitation only, immediately followed by an auction. We had only three days to prepare.

We headed to the van. Just before we went inside, Molly grabbed my hand. She squeezed it, and then kissed me on the cheek. "I forgive you," she said. "Now let's get on with it."

"Let's," I said. I slid open the door to the van. A cloud of smoke greeted us. The smoke finally dissipated enough to reveal Zane hunched over his nearly completed masterpiece.

"Is this what you wanted, Harry?" he asked.

I looked it up and down.

"It's perfect," I said.

I HAD ZANE write a confession: it told all about the hare-brained scheme, how it went awry, and how he returned to New York as a wanted man. He signed it. Molly and I also signed it as witnesses. The next day, when it was completely dry, I rolled up Zane's canvas and sealed it with tape. Zane signed his name over the seal. I then had him print the following words: "Only to be opened in the event of my death."

CHAPTER TWENTY

THE TUESDAY AFTER LABOR DAY was a quiet one down on the Jersey shore. I had Molly open an account at a local bank. Our plan was to extort Vincent and Teresa, and this was where the money was to be wired. Molly and I spent a lot of time together that day. Zane mostly stayed in the van. Not so much to keep out of view, but because he didn't want to spend any time away from Mittens. The only time he'd leave was to go to a pet store to buy her a new toy.

That night, Molly and I strolled along the boardwalk. Molly had the kazoo with her and hummed out tunes as we walked. It was a good way to avoid conversation.

"What song is that?" I asked.

"I don't know," she said. "But I can't seem to get the tune out of my head. No matter what I do, that's all I hear."

I was able to sympathize. No matter what I did, I couldn't get Julia out of my head. Until now. Now I couldn't get Molly out of my head. And I was going back to New York the next day . . . alone.

"I'm going to miss you, Molly."

"Then you should come to Mexico with us."

"I think that would be much too hard for me."

"Oh," she said with a glimmer of understanding. "I guess watching me and Zane together wouldn't exactly be your idea of a mentally healthy existence."

I just nodded, stopping myself from reminding Molly that she and Zane were only a couple in her mind. From the looks of it, Zane was either uninterested or oblivious, probably both. I wanted to spare her the pain of being cast off by Zane. I wanted to grab her wrists and look into her eyes and tell her about what really happened between Julia and me. Maybe she could learn from my misfortune, and then perhaps my often painful ordeal with Julia wouldn't have been in vain.

"Listen to me, Molly. I have to tell you something I've never told anyone else before. I'm only telling you this because maybe you can learn from my mistakes, and I would hate to see you get hurt the way I did. So here it is. The story of Julia and me. I'll begin at the beginning because that's the only way I'll be able to get through it. And please don't interrupt me. This is hard enough to say as it is.

"We met in elementary school. We were in a special class for the high I.Q. kids. Stayed in the same class all the way up through to high school, which took far fewer years for us than for the normal population. We stuck together because we were the only ones who'd talk to each other. So we became best friends. Neither of us ever dated anyone. Not only were we total nerds, we were also years younger than all the other kids in our grade. But I pined away for her all those years. We ended up going to the senior prom together, just as friends, of course. I tried to kiss her that night, and, because she was drunk, she let me. Sort of like the night you and I kissed on the Brooklyn Bridge, I suppose.

"After prom night, Julia shrugged off the kiss as if it were nothing. Just a harmless indiscretion on both our parts. We went to different colleges. Julia went uptown to Columbia, and I attended Cooper Union down in the East Village. Even though we were at opposite ends of the borough of Manhattan, I spent most of my time visiting Julia at Columbia. As a result, my academics suffered, despite the fact that I was a genius. I continued with that pattern even after we graduated; visiting Julia at her apartment and popping in unannounced whenever I could.

"But one day she wasn't alone. She had a friend—a *boyfriend*. Insanely jealous, I hatched a plan that ultimately resulted in their breakup. I won't go into details because they are too heinous to recount. But when the breakup finally occurred, she came running to me for comfort and support. She needed a shoulder to cry on and that shoulder was mine. My scheme had worked perfectly. She came to my apartment, smoked a truckload of cigarettes and went through two boxes of tissues. I took her to that bar on St. Marks Place. You know the one I'm talking about, right? Dark and dingy and perfect for feeling sorry for yourself. I got her drunk. Very drunk. Much drunker than she was on Prom Night when our lips first met. I was setting the stage for the long-awaited sequel.

"And what was my reward? She slept with the bartender as a rebound fuck. I was devastated. I was supposed to be the rebound fuck! Me! I was so pissed off about it that, in my drunken ramblings, I inadvertently confessed to her about my scheme that caused the split between her and her boyfriend. Obviously, our friendship was never the same after that. She'd rarely return any of my phone calls. And when she did, she'd make sure to call when she knew I was out and just leave a quick message on my answering machine. What was I to do?

"So the stalking began. I'd occasionally bump into her 'accidentally' every now and then, but most of the time I kept my distance. She never knew I was stalking her. Until the night I saw her meeting her old boyfriend. I followed them into a restaurant, 'accidentally' bumped into them and struck up a conversation. I casually mentioned to her boyfriend that I hadn't seen him since around the time that Julia fucked that bartender. Julia walked out abruptly. She left a message on my answering machine that night saying she never wanted to see my face again. That I was dead to her.

"So I stalked the two of them from afar. Became a substitute teacher because it was an easier schedule to fit in with the stalking. One night I followed them to a restaurant on the Upper East Side—fancy French one. I wasn't even properly dressed to sit at the bar, so I kept circling the block, trying to get a view of them through the windows. I finally got a good perspective in time to see lover boy pull a ring box out of his pocket and drop to one knee. To hell with improper attire. I emerged from the shadows and stormed past the maître d' to register my protestations. Among my impassioned ramblings were veiled threats, claims of my individual ownership of Julia, and several promises that they could expect to see me when they least expected it. I left the restaurant just before the police arrived. Julia got the restraining order the very next day. When I'd finally worked up the nerve to violate the order a week later, she was gone. Moved out, no forwarding address. I searched everywhere for her. Couldn't find her. As if she vanished into thin air. The only remnants I had of her were her cigarette butts. So if I was dead to her, then she'd be dead to me, too. I devised the urn to help stop the pain. As you can see, it hasn't worked very well.

"So, Molly, please don't head down this road with Zane. It can only bring you great suffering." That's what I should have told her on what may have been the last night I'd ever lay eyes on her. But instead, I remained silent while she tooted out an insipid and annoying tune on the kazoo. Pathetic.

Molly continued humming on the kazoo, then stopped herself and removed it from her mouth.

"This is driving me crazy," she said, and shoved the kazoo into my hand. "Here, hold onto this instrument of torture until I can get this damn song out of my head."

I pocketed the kazoo. Something to remember her by.

CHAPTER TWENTY-ONE

I PARKED THE VAN on Broome Street—a stone's throw from the Holland Tunnel—just in case a quick escape from Manhattan was in order. I tucked Zane's rolled-up canvas under my arm and walked casually to West Broadway and Spring Street. I stood across the street from the Reinhardt Galleries. I was in the very spot where I first saw Teresa Traut at the Dean Grimaldi splatter site. It was a wild ride thus far, and tonight promised to be no exception. I sipped a cup of coffee. I made a pact with myself that I wouldn't drink before this show. I'd learned my lesson after the last one. My hands shook, and I craved some whiskey to steady them, but I stayed true to my vow. I sipped more coffee, causing my hands to shake even more.

It was now eight-thirty. The guests had all arrived—even the fashionably late ones—and the bidding was going to begin shortly. I gave myself a quick pep talk and ascended the steps to the Galleries. Immediately I was intercepted by the Brat at reception.

"You're not on the list."

I flashed the rolled up canvas with Zane's signature and note prominently featured. The Brat's eyes widened.

She quickly excused herself.

"Wait here one moment, please," she said.

She returned exactly one moment later with Günther and Giselle in tow.

"What is the problem?" Giselle snapped.

I brought the signature to their attention.

"You get twenty percent," I said. "Just for doing nothing. My only condition is that you auction this piece before any of the others. Deal?"

Günther and Giselle exchanged glances. They seemed interested, but unsure.

"And you get to screw Teresa Traut as a bonus," I added.

Giselle grabbed my elbow and ushered me in.

The usual suspects were all in attendance. The Zane Burroughs groupies, the protégés, and the prize pigeons. They were huddled around Zane's new pieces. Teresa and Vincent stood to the side, presumably feeling at ease. They could hear the whispers and the rumors about who was willing to bid what and who was willing to outbid whom. Everyone wanted to own the very last pieces that Zane Burroughs had painted. Uncle Sal was also there, scoping out the room, just like a good lieutenant. But Ed was nowhere to be found.

So here I was. I had unleashed the latest hare-brained scheme and already there was a major glitch. I assumed Ed would be here. And that he would pounce on me and take me in for questioning right after the auction. That's where Zane's confession would come into play. But now, Uncle Sal would make sure I couldn't answer any questions. I decided to abort the mission and slip out before they noticed me. But just then, Günther clinked a wine glass to get everyone's attention. Teresa looked at Günther and caught sight of me. She flinched ever so slightly, and then composed herself. She waved to me, and then tapped Vincent on the shoulder and pointed me out to him. Vincent didn't wave. There was no turning back now. Instead, I approached my former co-conspirators for old times' sake. Uncle Sal joined the mix for good measure.

"I didn't realize you were on the list," Vincent said through clenched teeth. I was still shaking, but not from fear; it was the nasty combination of alcohol withdrawal and caffeine overload.

Teresa pulled him back. "Relax, darling. He can't do anything to us. Look at him. He's just a pathetic drunk."

Darling? So that's how it was. An encore performance of Julia and the bartender. I suppose I had suspected from the very first moment Vincent poured coffee for Teresa at The Last Stand but never accepted it. But there it was. Darling. She was playing him the way she played Ed and me.

Günther shouted over the crowd. "I have an important announcement. It is regarding Zane Burroughs's final work."

The crowd hushed.

"A new piece has surfaced." He waited for the predictable gasps from the crowd. I looked at Teresa. She still hadn't lost her composure.

"As a result," Günther continued, "we will auction the new piece first."

Günther motioned to me. "I now give you Mr.

Harrison Spangler."

I walked to the center of the room to the sound of murmuring. Deafening murmuring. The moment of truth was upon us. I hoped that Teresa and Vincent would take the bait.

"I hold before me the last thing Zane Burroughs painted." I held the rolled-up canvas over my head for extra effect. "It was sealed by Zane Burroughs himself, as you can see here by his signature on the tape that seals it. Above the signature are the eerie words: *Only to be opened in the event of my death.*"

I walked over to one of Zane's canvases on display and compared the signatures. I waited as each person present came forward and scrutinized the handwriting, leaving no doubt as to its authenticity. I looked at my watch.

"I will break the seal in exactly fifty-four minutes." I let the anticipation and longing set in. "And shortly after the viewing it will be auctioned."

A swell of would-be buyers mobbed me. I directed them to Giselle, and excused myself from the throng. I ambled over to Vincent and Teresa.

"Nice night, huh?" I taunted them.

"Where did you get that?" Teresa asked.

"From Zane," I said.

"You're bluffing," she said.

"Yeah," added Vincent. "It's pretty hard to paint without a fuckin' head."

"I got another package after you stole the other ones from me," I said. "It arrived the next day. Don't you just love the note and the way he signed his name across the seal on the canvas? Nice touch, huh? Should bring a hell of a price."

Teresa looked at Vincent.

"What does the painting look like?" Teresa asked.

"How should I know? It's sealed." I waited a beat and then said with dripping sarcasm, "Gosh, I sure hope it isn't anything incriminating."

"Why don't we take a walk?" Uncle Sal said.

"Fine," I said. "You can kill me if you want, but you're gonna have to disappear before that canvas is revealed. Which means you won't be able to stick around to collect any money from the rest of the pieces."

I let the words hang there. No one spoke for a minute. A minute that seemed like a lifetime. I finally broke the silence.

"Unless, of course, you would be willing to bid on it sight unseen."

"Fuck you, Harry," Vincent said. "You're scamming. I can see right through you. Look at the way you're shaking."

Vincent mistook my alcohol withdrawal and caffeine overload for nervousness. I countered quickly.

"If you're willing to take that chance, that's purely your decision. And Teresa's, too." I looked over to Teresa, but she was gone. She had made her way to the center of the room, and was clinking her glass to get everyone's attention.

"Friends," she began. "I understand how wonderful this new discovery of Zane Burroughs art work is; however, the police have classified the Zane Burroughs disappearance as 'a missing person' case at this time. The note that seals this canvas states that it should be revealed only in the event of his death, and until there is a body, or until he is reclassified as presumed dead, I'm afraid we just cannot reveal this painting."

There was a period of murmuring in the room. Günther and Giselle huddled together and gestured a lot. Finally, Giselle clinked her glass. I swallowed hard.

"After talking with my partner," Giselle said, "we must agree with Ms. Traut. It would be premature and therefore counter to this great artist's wishes."

The patrons responded with denial, anger and, finally, acceptance. The canvas would not be revealed tonight. Vincent nodded to Uncle Sal, who grabbed my elbow and pushed me toward the exit. Who could have predicted that a hare-brained scheme would misfire?

I DIDN'T THINK about my own looming demise. I thought about Zane and Molly; how I had let them down yet again. What was I thinking? Did I honestly believe I could extort the mafia? That I could outsmart Teresa in art dealing? Delusions of grandeur. Obviously I was not Lucy. Now Zane would never receive any money for his labors. And Molly. Although I was not a religious man, I prayed at that moment. Not for myself, but for Molly. For her happiness and well being.

Uncle Sal escorted me out of the Galleries.

"Where are we going?"

"The River," he said ominously.

We turned on Spring Street. We were only five blocks or so from the Hudson. As we approached Varick Street, I saw the idling traffic backed up from the Holland Tunnel. The fumes made me cough, and triggered my gag reflex. Too much coffee on an empty stomach. I heaved. Uncle Sal let go of me momentarily as I dropped to the sidewalk and emptied my stomach lining. After I had seemingly finished, I started to heave again; but this time it was purely theatrical. Suddenly I swung my arms as hard as I could right into Uncle Sal's ankles. He lost his balance, and I pushed him to ground. I gave him a quick kick in the ribs for good measure and then sprinted down Varick Street. I was only a couple of blocks from the Holland Tunnel. There was usually a traffic cop somewhere in the vicinity, and I was going to find him. But then I heard footsteps behind me. I began to run faster than I thought I could run. But it was to no avail. I felt a hand on my shoulder. It grasped me and then pulled me to the ground. I rolled over and looked up at my fleet-footed assailant. It was Detective Ed. He was huffing and coughing. Imagine how fast he could run if he weren't a smoker, I thought.

ED TENDED TO ME immediately. Within minutes of yanking me to ground, he had me set up with a shot of bourbon at a nearby bar on the corner of Spring and Renwick, a stone's throw from the Hudson River.

"Good thing you happened along," I said.

"Günther called me. He and Giselle were instructed to call if you ever came around the Reinhardt. We've got a lot of things to talk about."

"Hell, yes," I agreed. I dug out Zane's confession and threw it down on the bar for him.

I watched him read it, shaking his head up, then down, and then side to side. Then he ordered a beer.

"How do I know this is on the level?" he asked.

"Teresa and Vincent are selling his new pieces tonight at the Reinhardt," I said.

Ed inhaled a deep breath, then coughed a little. That endearing smoker's hack. I thought about Julia's urn. He took a gulp of his beer.

"I can't arrest you without taking Teresa down as well," he said.

"That's correct."

"And the victims of this scam are the people who bought the worthless art."

"Yes."

"But they wouldn't be victims if this never came to light. Their art would remain valuable, wouldn't it?"

He took Zane's confession and tucked it neatly into his pocket. And that was that. Ed was still under Teresa's influence.

"How come you didn't attend the show tonight?" I asked. "Didn't get an invite?"

"I'm working," he said.

"Drinking on the job?" I said, pointing at his pint of beer.

"I just went off duty."

"Then how come you're not at the show right now?"

He emptied his pint, and threw a twenty on the bar.

"Let's go," he said.

CHAPTER TWENTY-TWO

THE BIDDING was about to begin when Ed and I arrived at the Galleries. Teresa saw us come in and immediately greeted Ed with a big hug and kiss. I saw him melt. He was still under her spell. She was fully aware of this and she flashed me a big victory smile. She had all her bases covered. And Ed had sole possession of the only existing copy of Zane's confession. Another of my blundering oversights. How Lucy-ish of me. Teresa whispered something in Ed's ear, and Ed blushed. Then she gave him another kiss and went back to shmoozing with the clientele.

"A victimless crime, right?" I said to Ed.

"That's right," he answered.

Ed wasn't budging and I was desperate. So I tried a desperation play. Maybe I could use Ed's infatuation with Teresa to my advantage.

"I noticed that Teresa was a little friendlier than usual with Vincent tonight. I wonder if that's why she didn't invite you."

"Shut up, Harry."

"Maybe you could do something for her that only a cop involved in the Zane Burroughs investigation could do. Something that would make her very happy with your presence here."

I waited to see if Ed would take the bait.

"Go on," he said.

"Well," I said, setting the trap, "now that you know the score, what about giving Teresa a hand in upping the purchase price?"

"How would I do that?"

"Follow my lead."

I walked to the center of the room, and grabbed a glass for clinking purposes. Since the clinking sound was much more dramatic with an empty glass, I quickly imbibed the sweet sparkly liquid that was in it. Then I began clinking away.

"May I have your attention please?" I shouted over the murmuring crowd. "I only ask a moment of your time. What I am about to say may have some bearing upon the auction."

Günther, Giselle, Teresa, Vincent and Uncle Sal all looked very pissed. I continued.

"I have with me here, the detective assigned to the Zane Burroughs disappearance case. Isn't that right, Detective?"

"Um, yes," Ed said, somewhat unsure of himself.

"If you noticed, I used the term 'disappearance'— because that is how this case has been classified—as a disappearance. A missing person case. Isn't that right, Detective?"

"Um, yes. Yes that's correct," Ed said, catching on to my drift. Ed took it from there, playing right into my hands. "But it is my professional belief that Zane

Burroughs is most assuredly dead." Gasps from the crowd. Ed looked very pleased with himself, awaiting the reward Teresa would be giving him for helping her get a presumably higher sale price. I immediately extinguished his self-satisfaction.

"Based upon these statements," I said, "I propose that the canvas I brought tonight be unsealed and displayed immediately."

The crowd roared its approval, drowning out the protestations from Teresa and Vincent.

Ed looked confused. "What canvas?" he asked.

"You don't even know about the canvas?" Giselle jumped in.

Ed shook his head. Giselle ducked out and reappeared moments later with the canvas.

"And now, for one of the most exciting events in recent art history," she proclaimed, and broke the seal. The crowd pushed its way toward us with eager anticipation. Through the mob, I saw Teresa, Vincent and Uncle Sal push their way out the door, fleeing the scene. Giselle unrolled the canvas. She gasped. The crowd gasped. Even Ed gasped. Zane's newest piece certainly had a disarming effect on the viewer. It had originally been intended for Vincent and Teresa, but it seemed to work well in this scenario, too. It was a self-portrait of Zane. He had a huge grin on his face and he was swimming in a sea of hundred dollar bills. The wave formations of the hundred dollar bills spelled out the word "Suckers." This was presumably the money that we were to extort from Vincent and Teresa. It was intended to be a Lucy moment. But for this crowd, it took on a different perspective. They loved it. They believed it to be social commentary by a deceased artist about the valuation of art when the artist was living versus dead.

"Brilliant," one person said.

"Wonderful," said another.

"Ironically powerful and provocative," Giselle said.

The bidding was fast and furious. After Günther and Giselle took their twenty percent, the canvas cleared a hundred sixty-eight thousand dollars. I instructed them to wire the money into the account Molly set up at the Jersey shore. The other pieces weren't auctioned, since Teresa and Vincent had vanished from the show. No one seemed to notice.

Ed and I got a drink after the event. Now that he was complicit in a number of scams, he was in dire need of an explanation. I told him the entire story from beginning to end. How the Lucy episode fit in and how we thought Andrew Burroughs was Zane double-crossing us, and how it led to Vincent and Teresa calling in a hit. Ed didn't take it well. The Toronto police hadn't connected any of these dots, since the American and Canadian authorities weren't fully cooperating with each other's investigations.

"So what the hell do I do now?" he asked.

"You could solve the Andrew Burroughs murder," I said. "And then you can use that confession in your pocket to crack open the Zane Burroughs scam."

"But I'm complicit in it now. I gave that fucking speech saying he was dead."

"Only to see how Vincent and Teresa would react. And they fled the scene like the guilty murdering scam artists that they are. Get my drift?"

Ed nodded. "You're a very smart guy, Harry."

"All I ask is that you give me forty-eight hours for the money to get to Zane. He's really the big loser in all this. He can never return to New York, and he lost his brother."

"What about you? Gonna disappear?"

"Nah. I'm a New Yorker to the end."

"I know what you mean. Born and raised in Brooklyn," Ed said. "It's me and this city 'til death do us part."

We toasted the Big Apple, the city that Ed swore to protect.

EPILOG

ZANE AND MOLLY got the money and made a clean break to Mexico. They arrived in Juarez on Sunday, September 9th, two full days before the World Trade Center was attacked and destroyed. I got a post card from Molly in December. She wanted to make sure that I was okay. She also apologized for taking the money and running without waiting for me to take my cut, but reasoned that all the money was really rightfully Zane's, so I probably wouldn't care one way or another. She wrote that Zane was painting under a new identity, and living in blissful obscurity among the Mexican art community. She never mentioned if the two of them were "together" as a couple though, so I could only assume that they weren't. That's a detail she surely wouldn't have omitted. She signed the post card with a little smiley face inside the "o" in "Molly." Very appropriate, I thought.

Teresa turned evidence against Vincent and Uncle Sal. She sweet-talked Ed into pulling some strings with the D.A. to cut a deal, even though they had everything they needed to put all three of them away and didn't really need her testimony. Vincent and Sal went to jail for murder and conspiracy to commit murder. The fraud charges were sealed and never brought to light, so I was off the hook as well. Teresa bolted town as soon as the trial ended. She went to Seattle to revive her art career. Ed, humiliated by Teresa, retired from the police force and took a job teaching criminology at John Jay College.

The Reinhardt Galleries went out of business less than a year after the 9-11 attacks. Just about all of the galleries on West Broadway closed. A few years later, Günther and Giselle converted the upper floor of an old warehouse in Chelsea into Reinhardt Galleries II.

The Last Stand also went out of business, along with dozens of other SoHo/NoLita businesses that were hit hard by rough economic times. Tucker took his solo career to L.A. and became a contestant on a reality TV show, where he had the distinction of being voted off in the first episode.

The Asbury Park kazoo now shared a spot on my bookshelf with Julia's urn.

The two-year anniversary of mine and Molly's kiss was a warm clear August night. I placed the urn and the kazoo in the faux Gucci backpack I had purchased on Canal Street. I went for a long walk. I retraced the steps that Molly and I walked on the night of our kiss. I picked up a bottle of rum and a can of Coke, which added to the re-enactment. I walked halfway across the Brooklyn Bridge and turned to look at the Manhattan skyline, just as we did on that summer night. The skyline, of course, was horribly disfigured. I pulled Julia's urn out of the backpack. I mumbled a few incoherent words to myself, played a quick chorus of taps on the kazoo, and tossed the urn into the East River. Then I stared at the huge gap in the sky.

A few months later, there was a knock at my door. I was surprised to see Teresa Traut standing on the other side. She'd done a radical bleach job on her hair and was now sporting a short whitish-blonde bob. Apparently, it was a less-than-subtle attempt to distance herself from her previous life, and previous reputation; a hair cut and color was her quick remedy. I thought back to poor Mittens being transformed into Aldonza.

"I've got a proposition for you, Harrison," she said. "I think I can get myself back into the New York art scene, and you're just the person who can make it happen. How about a drink?"

I went to the kitchen to get some ice. She seated herself on the couch, perched right next to the Asbury Park kazoo on the bookshelf. When I returned with the ice bucket, I looked back and forth between the kazoo and the newly blonde Teresa Traut.

And I couldn't help but notice how much she looked like Molly.

ABOUT THE AUTHOR

RICH J. STONE is a native New Yorker, playwright, monologist and fiction writer. *Death Imitating Art* is his first novel.

Visit his website at www.richjstone.com.

www.ingramcontent.com/pod-product-compliance
Lightning Source LLC
Chambersburg PA
CBHW051832170626
46807CB00003B/1134